BELAJANE CRILLY

The Lady, The Thief, and The Warrior

First published by BelaJane Crilly (C. Andrews) 2021

St. Charles IL

Library of Congress Control Number: 2021909626

First edition

ISBN: 978-0-578-90273-9

This book was professionally typeset on Reedsy.
Find out more at reedsy.com

Herein is contained a devilish code,
A beastly dragon and a hoard of gold.
There are battles, dances, princes and kings,
Ice Cream and friendship and many more things.
If you are a lady with secrets dark,
If you are a warrior, brave of heart,
Or a thief with an impossible dream,
Or anyone at all, who loves to read,
Continue on and meet this varied cast,
Who'll keep you spellbound to the last.

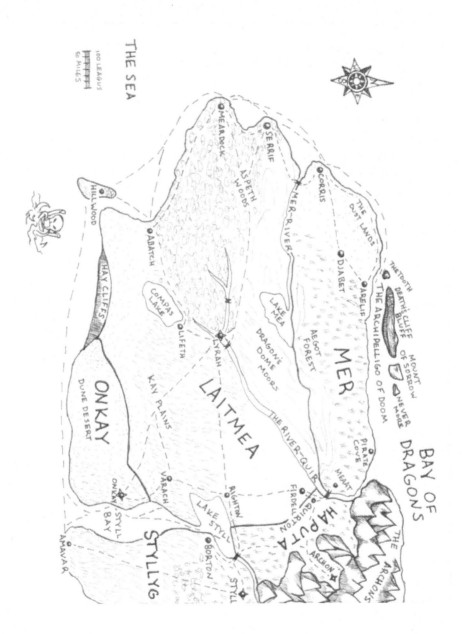

THE SEA

100 LEAGUS
50 MILES

MEARDOCK

SERRIF

ASPETH WOODS

HILLWOOD

ADATCH

HAY CLIFFS

COMPAS LAKE

OLIFETH

LYRAH

KAY PLAINS

ONKAY

DUNE DESERT

LAITMEA

VARACH

ONKAY STYLL BAY

AMAVAR

BORTON

LAKE STYLL

RIGHTON

FIRDELLTON

STYLL RIVER

ARCHON

STYLLYG

HAPUTA

THE RIVER QUIR

DRAGONS DOME MOORS

LAKE MEA

DJABET

ARELIF

AEGOT FOREST

MER RIVER

CORRIS

THE DUST LANDS

THE TOOTH

DEATH'S CLIFF BLUFF

THE ARCHIPELLIGO OF DOOM

MOUNT OF SORROW

NEVER MORE

MER

PIRATE COVE

MEAAT

BAY OF DRAGONS

THE ARCHONS

ii

Prologue

Year 111

The Continent of Eretz is in turmoil; there is great political instability in the land. Laitmea, the largest country, has been imposing strict taxes upon its neighbors. Onkay and Styllyg have already given in to their demands, but Haputa, the smallest of the near lands, refuses to pay. Haputians raid the borders frequently, continuing to resist despite rampant plague, which kills hundreds daily. Meanwhile, the Haputian Senate has been developing new plans of warfare. Laitmea's king, Darin the Terrible, fears their attacks, and sends word for several important records to be destroyed, lest they fall into the wrong hands. But not all goes according to plan...

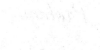

13

30 93 The Knight
The Knight Sir Brone was well renowned,
His name was sung in every town.
His tale was told by all the bards,
Children played him in their yards.
From where, you ask, came his fame?
How did he win such wide acclaim?
Here is the truth and if I lie,
Hang me up so that I die.
When under attack from the ship of a pirate,
Or caught in a city in the midst of a riot,
In battle against a thousand foes,
Or against every day nightmares and woes,
One response only Sir Brone had:
He turned around and ran like mad.
And if his armor weighed him down,
He collapsed as if dead upon the ground.
If his ship went down he sank,
In every battle he was outflanked.
If his horse went lame he left it there for dead.
There was not a mite of courage in his heart or head.

And so he was a laughing-stock,
He was roundly shunned and soundly mocked.
And when he asked how he got such a name,
He was told, "you sir, you only, are to blame."

From the diary of Trilliapa Gadrich

Year 114, 8th day of summer.

My name is Trilliapa Gadrich.

I will begin by saying that I am not an eloquent speaker or extraordinarily brilliant or quick and witty. In fact, the word that fits me best would be emotionless, but that's just not right either because I will try to let out my thoughts and feelings in this book. I've been thinking about how distant I am from sharing my emotions, and I've decided to give this journal a try. If these entries work, maybe I'll write more. Well, I haven't got anyone else to confide in, do I? Let me explain:

I might as well start my story with my age. I am eleven, and, according to my mother, very well read. Brone, my Father, is the cruelest person in all of Eretz. He used to be a Senator of some importance, until he took to playing cards and left the Senate in disgrace. Then, when he squandered all our family's money gambling, he took to drinking as well. In his drunken state, he assumed my mother and I had wasted the money. My mother had to work hard to keep us in the middle class, and Brone, (I refuse to call him "father") took all his anger out on us, for in his drinking he didn't realize we weren't poor. He would beat me for every little thing. He did the same to my mother.

A few weeks ago, we packed up so I could go fishing with my mother and Brone. He soon drank a little liquor, then a lot. In a fit of anger he struck my

3

mother, sending her tumbling to the side of the boat. He shoved her again. Screaming, my mother's skirts flew up and over the side, her golden blonde hair flying. Then, before my eyes, she disappeared under the waves.

I yelled for her 'til I lost my voice altogether. That was when I knew I had to escape. But I wasn't going to leave home unprepared.

That night I went down to the cellar where Brone kept the weapons he used to beat me, and looked long and hard for one of use. I searched until my eye fell upon a truncheon, a long, thin, curved, metal rod with a spiked cross guard. As soon as I spotted it, I knew I had to try it out. I took it up and felt its weight in my hands. It was heavy, but if I trained hard, I knew I could master it.

A week later, I packed only the necessities and took off. Where? I didn't know. But I found myself soon out of food and water and looking like a living skeleton. Maybe I wasn't as well prepared as I had thought.

I'd been wandering through town without any purpose when I found the orphanage. It seemed like a good enough place to stay. I certainly gives me enough to write about.

A day here is simple: wake up, eat, clean, clean, clean more, eat, bed.

I arrived early several mornings ago and came face to face with the ugliest, fattest woman I had ever met. She took one look at me, said a terrible oath that I never heard before, and hit me.

"Do as I say, and you won't get in trouble."

I was still a bit surprised and outraged at this greeting. My face stung where she slapped me, and I nodded automatically.

When I was shown my room, I was very glad I was good at hiding my feelings. The girls, perhaps thirty in all, were packed into a single small, dark, unclean room. I thought I saw a mouse run into a corner. The girls all looked like living skeletons themselves, so I fit in well.

A girl about my age glanced up when I entered and walked over to where I stood.

She was pretty in a different sort of way, her dirty blonde hair making a striking contrast to her bright green eyes. She wasn't exactly the kind of person that would turn heads in the street as my mother would, but in a way, she sort of reminded me of her.

"Hello," she said. Her eyes shone in delight at meeting someone new.

"Hi." I met her gaze with directness (or whatever you call it). Her hair looked a little like Mother's, yet she had a stronger build. This girl could hold her own in a fight.

"I'm Quipeneay," she said, looking me up and down, "but you can call me Quip."

I kept my blank expression. "I'm Trilliapa, but you can call me Trill."

Quip grinned and pulled something from her sleeve. I tried not to back away when I saw she had a knife. She flipped it up and down with ease.

"So," she smirked, "what brings you here?"

She's trying to test me, I realized, my mind racing, *she wants to see if I can hold my own*. And after years of being pushed around by Brone, I wanted to know that too.

I swallowed my sudden urge to run away from the threatening girl and faced her calmly. Before I could get a word in though, a shrill whistle echoed up to us. "Dinner!" The room erupted into a flurry of activity as every girl tried to beat the other down to eat. I simply followed the line, trying to act normal but sensing Quips eyes boring into me. *I'll prove myself to her. Very soon.*

* * *

13th day of summer

These days can be so boring! If it weren't for my recent escapade, I would try to escape. Just yesterday, I had a run-in with an older boy who was brutally forcing one of the other children to do his chores. He was tall and muscular, and I think I remember someone calling him Redge. He had a small boy pinned against the outside wall where the wash usually was hung, and honestly reminded me too much of Brone. This time maybe I could be more than a helpless bystander?

"Do it!" He growled angrily while the poor boy squirmed in vain against his grip. I set my load of laundry down on the dirt.

"Why don't you do it yourself?" I called over.

Redge whirled around, dropping the boy. Seeing me, he smiled a cruel smile and said, "You'd better scram, little girl or you'll help him."

He started toward me menacingly.

"Run, run!" he taunted.

I froze. My legs wanted to take his advice but my head told me to stay. He was almost upon me. Trying to buy time, I asked, "Why did you make him do your work? it's not right." I sounded like an imbecile, but couldn't think of anything else.

"It's not right." he mimicked, pushing his shaggy blond hair from his eyes.

By now he was practically upon me.

"Just leave him alone." I said, my voice shaking a bit.

He noticed and grinned. "Who's gonna stop me, you?"

I stepped forward, already feeling for my truncheon.

"Come on little girl! Come and get me!" he growled.

Crouching, he leapt at me. I knew what to do because Brone often used this method when taking me by surprise. I was ready. I pulled my truncheon out of my dress and stepped out of the way. However, he seemed to know that's what I'd do, for he reached out his arm and took me down with him. I slammed the truncheon down on his head viciously and jumped back up off him. He stilled abruptly and at first I thought I'd killed him, but I saw him breathing shallowly in pain. I hit him again, a knockout blow.

"That will bring him out of his misery," I said, smiling wickedly, "Or, at least 'til he wakes up."

Sighing with relief, I slipped my truncheon back into my dress. Then, turning, I walked to the doorway. A long brown dress caught my attention. Quip stood in my path, eyes alight,

"Good job." She said and followed me inside. I did it!

18

54 The pickpocket
Nimble fingers, sleight of hand,
Borrowed money, borrowed land.
Silent footsteps, dead of night,
Darkness hides me, so does light.
Jewels are taken, purse-strings cut,
Watches missing, silver-but,
They never feel, no one sees,
Gently does it, for the thieves.
Gentle fingers on the latch,
Softly, softly, thus I snatch.
Softly does it, on the stairs,
Silent as death in dragon's lairs.
Treasure hoarder, monster black,
Glorious golden things I lack.
No one knows that I am here,
No one knows they've aught to fear.
I'm here, gone, I won't be back,
I have treasure in my sack.
Glorious golden things I have.
Don't tell no one, I've been bad.

The Thief

15th day of summer

Today was an interesting day to say the least. With Quip as my ally, it seems like Redge has backed off a bit. However, the headmistress is a different story. She is a lazy, good for nothing lady who doesn't really care about any of the orphans she takes in, so long as she gets her money from the government. I recently noticed after she left the door to her room open, that she has a great big silk purse full of money. I snagged it and emptied just a few coins into my hand. As soon as I could, when Redge was busy tormenting children and Quip defending them, and the lousy headmistress hiding from both, I snuck out of the orphanage.

If I hadn't made a new friend or felt such loyalty to protect the weak, I might have made a run for it then and there when the headmistress was locked away in her room. Usually the city surrounding the orphanage is on the lookout for runaways but this time everyone was a little jumpy from a skirmish that got two Haputians killed. They didn't give me a second glance.

I soon found a small group of children gathered around a stall. Some were holding little cups of mushy white stuff. Since it was so popular, I decided to try it. The man at the stall asked how many scoops I wanted so I said four. You know, four little spoonfuls of mush. Well, it didn't work that way. I found myself holding a small pail of vanilla ice cream, for that is what it said on the sign. The rest of the children were staring wide-eyed at me. The

8

man said that would cost me five silver crowns. I had only grabbed four.
Desperately, I looked around for a solution. A man walked up next to me
to order two scoops, and without thinking, I nimbly stuck my hand in his
pocket and pulled out the silver coin. He didn't even look my way. I handed
over the money and took my pail of ice cream back.

I suddenly felt confident in my abilities. As people walked by, they looked
so distracted, I made myself a challenge, seeing how many coins I could take
from wealthy peoples' pockets and put into the poorer peoples' pockets. I
was never caught which only made my confidence grow. And why shouldn't
it? I've had to slip coins away from Brone more times than I can count. This
way I'm not just helping myself. Maybe somebody else can get a meal out
of this too. By the time I got back to the orphanage, all but one scoop of ice
cream was eaten. The scuffle Redge had created had long since passed and
Quip jumped at me from the back doorway.

"Where have you been?" I held up my pail of ice cream,

"For you. One scoop left." she eyed it,

"How much did you eat?" I shrugged,

"Three scoops." Her mouth twitched,

"Looks like I'll get your dinner tonight"

I glared "Humph! Then I won't give you this!"

I held up two coins in front of her nose. Her eyes gleamed and she snatched
them from my hand.

"Hey!" I laughed. But the joke was on her for that night, when she reached
into her pocket for them, they'd be gone.

* * *

15th day of summer

Last night at dinner, my stomach felt horrible and Quip was gleefully eating
my portion while I moaned and groaned. She was licking up the last bit when
two boys started shoving each other. Quip immediately said to stop, but then
Redge joined in and she reached in her pocket for her knife. I was practically
under the table in misery when Quip screamed in rage. Everyone froze except

me. I slid further and further down until I was concealed.

"WHO TOOK MY KNIFE?" her eyes flashed dangerously and even Redge cowered in fear. Not me.

"Isn't it in your pocket?" I muttered from under the table.

I saw the kick coming and dodged, whacking her with my truncheon at the same time. Meanwhile, I slipped her knife in her other pocket.

"Look." a younger girl pointed. "There's your knife!" I slid up from the table, truncheon out but it wasn't necessary. Quip saw it and exclaimed in surprise.

"Oh, Trill! I thought... Oh never mind. I'm sorry about kicking you. You didn't deserve it." I sniffled a little (Quip's not the only one who plays tricks on people,)

"It's ok. It didn't hurt ...much." Later that night when we were lying in bed, Quip began to complain of hunger pains even though she'd had both our meals.

"Here." I handed her one mushy apple, and a few walnuts.

"Wow. Where'd you get this? I guess I'll need my knife to cut the bad spots off." she said, reaching for where she kept it. I slipped my hand up to my skimpy pillow case and handed the blade to her. I'd swiped it after dinner. She started up in bed.

"Wait, what?" she said, a bit loudly in her disbelief. I just rolled over and fell asleep.

* * *

16th day of Summer

"A raid." These words were spreading fast through meal time. It seems that Haputa's soldiers are going to attack the Laitmean border guards. Quip ate her dinner very fast and signaled for me to do the same. Then, she went to bed. Seriously? I ate fast just to watch her sleep? Well, I'm going to bed now. Goodnight.

* * *

Later

What a night! Close to midnight, I felt Quip shaking me. I sat up groggily.

"What's your greatest dream?" she asked.

I sighed, "To go back to bed..."

"Hurry!" she glanced about frantically.

Did I dare tell her about my deepest held secret? She had been a good friend these past few days, but I'd never told anyone about my ambitions, not even my mother. Why was she asking... and then it hit me. A Raid! I knew the answer she wanted to hear, and breathed a sigh of relief. I'd be a bit embarrassed to tell her about my other greatest dream, I just know she'd laugh.

So I said, "To fight in Haputa's army."

It might seem odd to some that I want to fight in the army, but I've always thought that defending my country was quite a noble cause. Also, I know Brone wouldn't approve, and a bit of me still wants to spite him. Well, most of me really.

"That's My dream too." She grabbed my hand.

"What?" I began when she led me outside and towards the fighting. (Through the boys room too! I was convinced that Redge would wake up, but he didn't.)

"Trill, fight for our Senate. Fight for Haputa!" She raised her dagger in the air and ran into the thick of the fight, pulling me behind her.

I did fight. I fought to see another sunrise. But I also fought for Haputa.

* * *

23rd day of Summer

Not much is going on. I don't know what to say. I've been on a few raids, but right now it's pretty much a stalemate. There are all kinds of nasty rumors here about Laitmea. People say that their king, Darin, is just about the worst person ever. Well, my own father was the worst person ever, and he used to

11

be a Senator for dear Haputa herself. I guess that's how it is in war though. And after seeing the skirmishes, I'll believe anything about Laitmeans. They'd even kill a man who's trying to surrender.

TRILLIAPA
GADRICH

From the diary of Redgenold Peterson

41st of winter, year 112.

I bought a little book and pen today, cheap things both, but more than I should have spent. I've only a few coins and I like not to spend them, as they're all my mother left me, but I think she'd want me to do this.

She used to write her life's story in letters to her brother Efin, begging forgiveness, but she never got a reply, and now her letters are unfinished, as she died giving birth to me. The woman she left me with says she was not a good sort-she'll flog me for writing this, but I will finish my mother's story now. Her brother shan't get the end of it, I fear, but as it was he that was supposed to look after me, and he left me to this miserable orphanage, that doesn't concern me much.

My mother was not a moral woman. I have come to understand that she killed a man, tho' how or why, I cannot say. My father was from Styllyg. He died even before I was born, killed in the service perhaps a week after I was conceived.

After his death, my mother returned to a town near her home, ill as death, and when her brother turned her out, she was forced to leave me to the orphanage. I was born early, and the strain of it, after the sickness, killed the poor woman. As I am her only son, the end of her story is my story. I'll write it as a diary, not letters, for my uncle has proved unresponsive.

I live under the care of the same orphanage matron my mother left me with when she died. It has now been nearly sixteen years since… I learned to read and write from an older boy, before he died of the plague three years ago. Half the children in this place are here because of it. I've never been sick with it before, and I'm grateful for it. Plague has made many a beggar blind. It is mostly past now, but when I was six and seven years old, around the year one hundred and twenty-two, not a day went by without someone dropping dead of it. There were bodies in the street, for no one wanted to bury them.

Life is not pretty here. You eat, you sleep, you work until you die. In one year, I'll be apprenticed to some tradesman or other, and in another twenty, I'll be dead. Indeed, my mother's legacy is not a happy one.

The one thing that would bring me joy is just now out of reach. I hesitate to write of it, even to an uncle that will never read it, and my mother, dead, but I feel I must, else I burst.

Her name is Quip. A common, plain name, but beautiful. She came here seven years ago, when the land was in the grips of the plague. It took her father, her mother, and I think a little sister too, but she doesn't speak of that. She was still woefully thin and wracked with pain when she was brought in, and did naught but sob and clutch her rag doll- even when the fever left her. I think she was able to stay in the corner because everyone felt too sorry for her to make her move. I had only just turned eight then, and still had in my possession something of my mother's - a little knife. It was fine work, but I hadn't a clue how to use it. She was just sitting there in a daze, all skin and bone and long ragged blond hair, so I paid her no mind. There was a younger boy there, perhaps six years old, and I took out the knife to give him a fright. I was taunting him with it, and I felt her eyes on me. I had mimed throwing the blade, and she got up. It was the first time anyone had heard her speak, and we all could have died of surprise.

"Don't torment him! It's cruel."

She was only seven years old, and still thin as a skeleton, but when she hit, she hit hard. She was wiry and strong, and once she had hold of my knife hand, she wouldn't let go. Getting beaten is bad, but getting beaten by a little wisp of a girl is worse. I knew that if I let her win, I'd be fighting tooth and nail for the rest of my life trying to live it down. She kneed me in the stomach and

15

I let go of the knife. There was no getting it back now. That knife replaced her doll. She knew how to use it, and when she grew a little stronger, she devoted herself to it. The knife, and the dream. Her one love is Haputa. I watched her kill a man once, in the heat of a skirmish. The matron forbids us from leaving the orphanage when there is a fight with a border guard, but Quip often sneaks out the window on the boys side of the dormitories where the glass is broken - she is the sort that the old woman warns about. Like my mother.

Quip has made my life a blistering hell, but I cannot deny, I admire her. Everyone does - the children, the people she steals from, the Laitmean soldiers she kills, her best friend - a little slip of a girl named Trill. Hate her or love her, they all admire her. When exactly admiration turned to love, I cannot begin to fathom. The little children laugh when she beats me, and the shame of it burns, but not so much as the other fire. I feel a thrill every time she walks by. I burn like a hot ember every time she wrestles me to the ground. She might well have laid me open with her knife for how my chest hurts. I hate her for it - I love her.

* * *

1st of spring, year 111

There was a raid today, though Quip at least stayed inside for this one, Laitmea tightens the noose. I hope they do not try to move in further to our lands - we can ill afford the loss of crops, not to mention it would drive Quip mad. They say king Darin of Laitmea killed his older brother to take the throne. That's just a wild rumor, but if it's true, I don't want to think of what he'll do if Haputa falls.

* * *

3rd of spring

Today an old man died of plague. He used to beg at the corner across from here. The illness strikes down many, even when it is not so bad as in the past.

16

* * *

4th of spring

She taunts me - Quip. That damned Quip. Perhaps those who didn't know me would think me a menace, but then I see her and I go to pieces! I'm nothing to her, I know, just a minute annoyance, a fly. Sometimes I provoke her just to feel her hands on me. Yanking my shoulder out of joint.

* * *

8th of spring

I spent another night in the cellar. I do not like rats much, but it is the damp cold that I despise. There is not enough to eat, nor enough candles to write by. I hate this place.

* * *

11th of spring

Quip. I fear I say her name in my sleep. Goodness knows what would become of me if the other boys heard. As the biggest, I get the bed most nights, but I might well be mocked out of it if the little ones think I've turned into a ladies man.

The Thief

Year 111, 16th day of spring

Wow, I can't believe I haven't written in three years! So much has happened. I'm now fourteen. My blue eyes have been going green in different lights and my once golden locks have turned to a muddy blonde. I have just gotten a new dress. It is dark blue. The headmistress told me it was an early gift for my birthday. Ha! Birthday gift indeed! It comes down to my ankles and the waistline is enormous. It looks like one of her old dresses. I have to use a rope for a belt or it will never stay on.

Quip smirked when she saw me in it.

"New dress?" she asked.

"It wasn't my choice," I retorted.

She grinned, "I can tell."

From the diary of Quipeneay

Year 111, 18th day of spring

Hello, new diary. My name is Quip, I'm fourteen, and I've lived in an orphanage on the west side of Quirton, Haputa since my parents died of the plague when I was seven. I know my best friend Trill has kept a diary on and off for years, but this is the first time I've tried it. I'm guessin' my entries will be shorter then hers. Generally, I talk more then I write. I like fire and theft, and teachin' bullies not to beat up little kids, but most of all, I love my country. HAPUTA FOREVER !!!!!!!!!

Laitmea's got no right to take our land or hard earned money, and some day, I'm gonna tell them that. I've always wanted to join the army, but it's not proper for a girl to fight, and I'm too young, so I just sneak out and join them on raids when nobody's lookin'. It's really more of a lot o' farmers with pitchforks then an army, and not too many of them get killed, least by the standards of yer average war. Anyways, I'm keepin' a diary now, 'cause I lost a bet with Trill on who could pick more people's pockets in a day, so I have to write every week at least.

For a whole year.

Bye for now.

* * *

20th day of spring.

Today was very interestin'. It started off with Trill jumpin' on me, and ended with a fight. Trill said that she was hungry, which she does every day, so we went lookin' for food. Well, what should we find in the nice district but a man sellin' ice cream. I distracted him while Trill filled her pockets full. It might've been better if Trill hadn't filled her pockets wit spiders first tho'. To make things even more interestin, we overheard a Senate meetin'. I probably shouldn't write any more tho, 'cause Redge is lookin' my way, the filthy bully. He thinks he's top dog 'round here, but everyone knows that's me and Trill. Loyalists to Haputa get respect 'specially 'cause we beat on anyone who goes 'round saying that Laitmeas' got any right to take anythin'. The matron is the only one who gets less respect than Redge.

Redge ain't here now, so I'll finish. We went down the first alleyway on the left of high street, and stopped in the back of an old house to eat, when we heard voices, almost like we were at the cellar door when the matron is down there tellin' some kid to behave. Turns out that we could hear real well if we listened at the keyhole. It was the Senate, which was interestin, cause Laitmea is out to get those guys, and they ain't supposed to be meetin'. (You know they even say Laitmea's king killed his own brother to get the throne.) Like I said. Laitmeans are all scum.

The Senate had some secret plans, good ones too, but I ain't dumb enough to write them down. Hopefully Trill ain't either. When we got back to the orphanage, we found Redge bossing 'round some little ones. Trill told him what she thought o' that in no uncertain terms. Her truncheon even backed her up. 'Reckon she'll have to spend the night in the cellar for it. I've got to go break her out. I think there'll be a raid tonight.

The Thief

20th day of spring

I turned fifteen today. Goodness, that sounds old. Quip helped me steal ice cream, and we both stuffed our faces. I think it tastes better when it's not paid for.

Oh, and I played a trick on Quip - Stuck a spider in her serving for her! Nice and fresh and squishy. There was something else interesting too: the Senate. I'll never write down a word of what they said, in case somebody finds this book. Haputa would be ruined if anyone knew about the new weapon!

Anyway, I'm in the cellar now, but I hear some tapping in the passage... better go now. My fight with Redge wasn't that exciting anyway. Write more later.

Redgenold

20th of spring, year 111

Trill- Quips' friend- once again set upon me with her truncheon. I had hoped Quip would see fit to discipline me, but she seemed too preoccupied. The matron caught us scuffling in the hall, and tossed us both in the cellar, but she dare not take Trill's truncheon. She's quite scared of the girl, and even tries to placate her - just a few days ago she gave her a new dress, though I must say it does nothing for her figure. I don't know what Matron thinks to accomplish. Trill will keep fighting and picking pockets 'til the day she dies.

14

49 Snow
Do you love to walk in snow?
Listen to the cold wind blow,
See the world all covered in white,
Feel the frost's cold, icy bite,
Taste the snowflakes on your tongue,
And at last, when you are done,
Return to your cozy house,
Settle down, snug as a mouse,
To sweet smells of warm cocoa,
Knowing that you'll never go
Outside again 'till spring?

From the diary of Lady Ettalara Annalee of Firdell

~∞∞∞~

21st day of spring, year 111

My name is Ettalara, and I am fourteen years old. I grew up in the Eastern part of Laitmea, with my parents, Cornelius and Hillena. My childhood was a happy one. My father was a member of parliament, and as a result, we were quite wealthy. I had a very good education for a girl. I studied everything from music and art to science and fencing, and I was also trained in the domestic arts, like needlepoint. I taught myself how to cook by sneaking into the kitchens at night, for my mother did not approve of a girl of my station cooking. I enjoyed it, however, and soon my mother relented, and I was permitted to help Cook, once my studies were finished.

I had two maids, and several instructors, although father taught me fencing and mother helped me with music and needlepoint. Our home was large, and so I had a parlor, bedchamber, and playroom when I was younger, all to call my own, as well as a small rose garden just beneath my balcony window. At night, I used to leave my window open, so the breeze would carry the sweet scent of flowers into my bedchamber. Of course, if Mother caught me, she would make me close the window for fear I would die of consumption.

We often took trips to the country, or to the lake, whenever father could get away from his pressing business. We had a summer home on the lake

24

and stayed with some of father's friends in the country. I loved those little excursions, for then, I needn't worry about studies and the days were spent picnicking or riding, reading novels, or strolling through the abundant grounds.

It was on our way home last year, from one of our autumn visits to the lake, that we were caught in a sudden blizzard. Where it came from, no one seems to know, but suddenly the wind blew fierce and the sky went gray and cold. Snow began to fall from the heavens, and not in little flurries. It snowed as I had never seen before. It was so white, that from inside the carriage, we could see neither horses nor driver.

Then, suddenly, the carriage rocked violently and stopped. The driver's white-streaked face appeared at the window to explain that the wheel had come off. He announced he would try to fix it, and Father stepped out to help him, but it was no good. They could hardly see anything, and their fingers were numb with cold. Meanwhile, it grew colder and colder inside the carriage and Mother and I snuggled in close, trying to keep ourselves warm. A few moments later, Father opened the door and told us we would have to walk home, although we were nearly five miles away. Mother bundled me up tightly, and then we set out into the bitter cold.

We reached home several hours later, half frozen, and took immediately to our beds. I recovered quickly, but father died only two days later. We tried to keep the news from mother, as she was still weakened, but somehow she found out and died of shock. It's true: in just five short days, I lost both my parents.

I really don't remember much of those next few weeks. There was a funeral which I attended, but sat through in a daze. I wished desperately that it was all a dream, an ugly nightmare from which I would awaken at any moment. Instead, father's lawyer arrived. He announced that my father had many debts and we would have to sell our home and belongings. I sat there silently, trying to understand. They would take our home, just like that? What would become of me? The lawyer answered that next. He had tallied up the cost of our valuables, but there was still a significant sum left to be paid. As a result, I would become a servant for at least five years, or until the debts were paid.

25

This plan was to be carried out immediately, but a few of the more loyal servants convinced the man to withhold his sentence, at least for a few months, while I recovered. I was still weak from the sickness, you see, and grieved because of my parents' deaths. The lawyer agreed, rather reluctantly, and I was very grateful. One of my maids, the cook, and a coachman stayed with me, cooking my meals, and helping me to recover. I am truly grateful for their service, and I told them so many times, for there was no other way I could repay them until I came of age. None of the items or money in the house belonged to me anymore. Because I would be going into service, my maid taught me to sew. They were all very gentle and patient with me. If I ever regain my fortune, I shall reward each of them handsomely.

Finally, the day came when my belongings began to be taken from me. First the furniture in the parlors and bedchambers, then the horses and carriages, and even the finest clothes from our closets. Then I was informed that I would be leaving the very next day. So I fled. Not because I was a coward, but on account of the book.

I truly have no idea how the book came into my Mother's possession, but I found it among her belongings the day after the funeral. It seems she wanted me to find it, for in the front, there was a note addressed to me. It said that I knew to whom the book belonged and that I must get it there as quickly as possible. It belongs to my king. The contents of the book I shall not reveal in these pages, for I am already putting myself at too great a risk. I suppose it can be gathered from my previous words that the book is very important, yet I shall try not to reveal any more than that.

At any rate, I realized that this book must be taken to my king at once. So, I made up my mind to escape and attempt to return it to him. I have never actually met him, but I have heard that he is fair, if a bit stern. There are all sorts of nasty rumors about him that the Haputians have started (they've even gone so far as to claim that he *murdered* queen Elisabet!). I don't believe any of them for a second.

That night, I packed my satchel with food, a small amount of money, a comb, a map, my little knife, a telescope, some sewing supplies, and of course, the book. I put on my warmest traveling dress, for I knew the nights would be cold, and began my journey.

I had been traveling for several days, when I was caught in the raid. My country borders several others, including one called Haputa. The smallest of the neighboring countries, Haputa has been a trouble maker for as long as I can recall. They are always picking fights with the Laitmean soldiers guarding the border and as a result, very few people from my country live near those parts. At any rate, the Haputian soldiers won this skirmish, and captured me. I had to tell them I was from their country, or they could have killed me. My plan was to make it look like I was heading toward Haputa, but then circle around and go back to Laitmea. But the soldiers must have been suspicious of my accent, for they followed me from a distance. I had no choice but to journey further and further into enemy territory, hoping to lose them.

When it began to grow dark and I still had not shaken them, I began to think about what I should do. It would be too dangerous for me to attempt to sleep on the streets, for I'd heard robbers lurked everywhere in Haputa. I needed someplace safe. I was wandering aimlessly (but trying not to look like it) through a small border town when I came upon a dim, two-story building with a sign that read "Orphanage." I hesitated. Once in, it would be quite difficult to get out. But I could think of no other option. With all the boldness I could muster, I walked up to the front door and knocked— I must go.

The Thief

21st day of spring

A new girl is here! Quip and I were up in the dormitory when we heard some soft steps and the front door opening. We got down the ladder to see a girl around Quip's age (fourteen) standing at the door. Unfortunately, Redge beat us there.

"A new girl," he said, cracking his knuckles with glee.

"Will you let me through?" she asked, eyeing him up. She had long brown hair, bright, piercing blue eyes, and a slender frame. She had such an authoritative voice that I forgot her situation while surveying her.

"Leave her alone," Quip growled at Redge. He glared at Quip and rolled his eyes.

"Or," she added, pulling out a familiar object, "would you like to meet your old friend?" Redge studied the knife, then backed away.

"May I come in?" the girl asked, also surveying Quip's knife (only in obvious alarm).

"Sure," Quip shoved her knife up her sleeve and gave the girl one of her famous lopsided grins.

"I'm Ettalara," the girl said.

"I'm Quip and this is Trill." Ettalara turned to me as if seeing me for the first time. "You can just ignore her," Quip joked, as if I talked too much, because, as I said before, I'm a girl of few words. I pushed my dirty blonde hair out of

28

my eyes and nodded greetings. I started for the ladder and climbed up. Quip and Ettalara followed.

"This is the girls' room," Quip explained. Ettalara seemed shocked as she stared at the room. I secretly wondered if that was how I looked when I arrived three years ago.

"So," she said as she tossed her bag to the floor, "what do you do around here?" Quip and I exchanged glances. Everyone in Haputa knows what it's like for orphans.

"We eat, clean, and sleep," Quip answered.

"You clean?" Ettalara looked skeptical. "You *clean?*" she asked again.

"Yep," said Quip, getting annoyed.

"Well it certainly doesn't look like it."

Suddenly, a bell rang and Ettalara jumped. I smiled.

"*That's* the dinner bell."

Ettalara's eyes widened. "Usually it's the other way around."

Quip and I looked at each other again. This girl is *not* from here.

The Warrior

Year 111, 21st day of spring

Today progressed as normal 'til bout an hour before sundown. Redge was makin trouble as always, this time for a new kid. She said she's from near the border, and that she was an orphan. My, is she strange! She talks more like Trill than me, but really she don't talk like anyone 'round here. She's dressed all fancy too, so I wonder what she's doin' in a poor town. I don't know what Trill thinks, but I reckon she's hidin' somethin'. Donno what.

Went on another raid last night. Think I killed a guy. Not sure, but if I did, he was Laitmean. I think that's alright? I only ever kill Laitmeans, and that's cause they deserve it. I try not to kill anyone else, least-ways not if they don't support Laitmea, that's just as bad and worse than bein' one of 'em. Still feel sorry for him tho. Must be hard getin stabbed by a girl. I'd drop dead on the spot from sheer embarrassment if it was me.

Redgenold

22nd of spring, year 111

The most odd girl I have ever met turned up yesterday evening. I heard some tapping on the door, and opened it to see her standing there, looking like she'd come to buy the place. I thought of smacking her to the other side of the street, but Quip thought she should be let in, and I'll not argue with her when she flashes my mother's knife. The girl seems to have befriended Quip and Trill after a manner- She's scared stiff that they'll kill her in her sleep, but grateful that they let her in. Quip clearly thinks the new girl is beneath her- though judging by her clothing quite the opposite is true- I admire Quip's self-confidence, but I wonder if it isn't misplaced. Something about the girl rubs me the wrong way. Trill is as hard to read as ever, but if I were to hazard a guess, I'd say she trusts the new girl as much as she does a rattlesnake. I do like that Quip is so easy to read. Trill hides her emotions so well that it's hard to tell when she's going to strike.

QUIRTON

The Lady

24th day of spring

Obviously, the orphanage is where I am now. It is only my third day here. Things did not turn out quite as I expected the night I knocked on the door, but let me explain...

The door opened, to reveal a rather tall boy, blocking the entrance. He swept his unkempt strawberry-blond hair aside and cracked his knuckles.

"So, a new kid," he grinned menacingly.

"Will you let me in?" I was in a near panic. If this boy would not let me through, the soldiers trailing me would put two and two together and I was as good as dead.

"Let her alone, Redge," said a voice from behind the door, "or do you want to meet your old friend?" Redge glanced at whoever was speaking and his eyes widened slightly. Then, to my utter surprise, he stepped aside!

"Come on in," said the voice, and I stepped inside only to find myself face to face with a girl holding a very sharp knife. She slipped it up her sleeve and grinned at me. She had short blonde hair and green eyes and seemed to be about my age.

"I'm Quip," she said, "and this is Trill. You can just ignore her," she added with a laugh. It was then that I noticed Quip's companion, a smaller girl with curling caramel locks and blue-green eyes. At first, I thought them to be sisters, but I found out later that this was not the case.

33

"I'm Ettalara," I offered, glancing about. The place was dirty, with cobwebs in the corners and mud streaked on the floor. We were standing in a kind of foyer, to the left was a door with faded letters that read "Headmistress." To the right, I could see into a kind of dining hall, with three tables, each having two long benches, enough to sit ten children on each, I guessed. Against the farthest wall in that room was a ladder.

"You nobility? That's a pretty nice dress," Quip remarked.

"Oh, yes," I replied, a little too quickly.

"Are you from Haputa?"

"Of course." Quip looked a little doubtful, so I decided to change the subject. "Will you show me to the bedchamber?"

"Follow me," said Quip, with an amused glance at Trill. We entered the dining hall and ascended the ladder. Upon reaching the top, I beheld the girls' dormitory. It was dark, grimy, and thoroughly unsanitary. There were only two narrow cots, pushed up against the wall, and for the others, a pile of folded blankets lay in the dusty corner. There was one window, overlooking the entrance. Trill and Quip must have seen me through it to have gotten down so quickly.

I plopped my bag down on the uneven wooden floor and surveyed my companions.

"So, what are the rules around here?" I inquired.

"No skipping on chores, no stealing food, no one down stairs before five in the morning or after eight at night, no fighting, and no weapons," Quip recited. Then she grinned. "We break those last two rules a lot."

Fighting and concealed weapons. I was regretting my coming here more and more.

"And the punishments?"

"A night in the cellar, usually," Quip replied. Suddenly, a bell rang. All the other girls in the room jumped up and hurried downstairs.

"What is that?" I asked, alarmed.

"Dinner," said Trill with a grin.

I descended the ladder and made my way into the dining hall, which was quickly filled with rowdy boys and girls, probably close to sixty in all.

I sat between Quip and Trill at supper, which consisted only of greens and a piece of bread. I was famished, however, and quickly finished the meal, though it wasn't very good. We went back upstairs for bed, and Quip offered to get me a cot since it was my first night here. I told her I'd slept on the floor before and I'd do it again, which seemed to surprise her. But she shrugged and didn't argue, so I laid down under a strange smelling blanket and fell asleep for the first time in days.

* * *

28th Day of Spring

I always suspected my new companions were slightly audacious, but I didn't realize how much so until just last night. We had heard sounds of a fight, some ways off, but close enough to make me uneasy. I went to bed as usual, but couldn't fall asleep for fear of the outcome of the skirmish. About an hour or so later, I heard stirring from across the room. Slowly peeking out from under my blanket, I saw Quip standing up cautiously, and then shaking Trill.

A moment later, they were sneaking across the floor, stepping carefully to avoid the creaky floorboards. As soon as they were out of sight, I stood up and followed them. They went down the hall, and then entered the boys room! I was shocked! I would not follow them in there, no matter how curious I was. Then, it occurred to me that they must have left the building from that room! I raced to the nearest window just in time to see them drop from the broken window on the boy's side to the ground below. Then, pulling out their weapons, they rushed off towards the battle, which still raged fiercely.

I soon lost sight of them, but did not move from my post by the window. I waited there until things quieted and I knew the battle had ended. Shortly thereafter, two dark figures came into view. Quip and Trill! I was relieved, but slightly alarmed. If they were willing to sneak out at night to fight in a true, dangerous battle, not a petty children's' fight, I knew they would do almost anything.

Suddenly, Trill pointed directly at me, and Quip looked up too. I ducked out of sight and hurried back into the girls' dormitory before they reentered.

A few moments later, I heard the creak of the door and knew they were creeping back to their places. I relaxed and fell asleep, though only for an hour or so.

I awoke when it was still dark, and found Quip and Trill already in a whispered discussion. I tried to listen in, but found I couldn't, they were too quiet. So instead, I sat up and yawned. I rubbed my eyes, trying to fully wake up. If there's one thing I learned in the orphanage, it's that from the moment you wake up until the moment you go to sleep, you must be alert and keep your wits about you.

"You saw us last night, didn't you?" Quip demanded, the moment she saw I was up. My heart raced. I didn't want to tell her the truth for fear of her reaction, but I could see there was no point in lying.

"Yes, I did. What on earth were you thinking? You could have been killed!"

"I *told* you, Ettalara," Quip replied, exasperated, "We're loyalists!" Trill nodded in agreement. I rolled my eyes.

"There's a difference between being loyal and being just plain foolish!" I retorted.

Quip, meanwhile, was studying me closely. I shifted uncomfortably under her gaze.

"Where are you *really* from, Ettalara?" she asked. My heart quickened again.

"Here, of course. Why do you ask?"

"Well, for one thing, your accent is Laitmean. And for another, you seemed upset at the thought of me and Trill fighting against the *Laitmean* soldiers." I did not like the way this conversation was going. I needed an escape, and quickly.

"I'm going down for breakfast," I said, rising abruptly. Trill and Quip glanced at each other as I descended the ladder.

"It's too early. You'll get in trouble," Quip whispered after me, but I payed her no mind. It was worth getting in trouble if it meant this conversation would come to an end. I crept into the dining hall and sat sideways on the bench, drawing my knees to my chest and laying my chin upon them. I sat there thinking for only a few moments before I heard footsteps on the ladder and Quip and Trill joined me. I hadn't counted on that. Well, there would be no avoiding it now. They sat down next to me, and after a slight hesitation, Quip asked,

"So, you really are from Laitmea?" I nodded, miserable. Trill drew in a deep breath, and when I glanced over at her, she looked very angry. Quip just nodded, as though something had been confirmed.

"Are you going to turn me in?" I asked after a pause.

"That depends. What are you doing here?"

"I was caught in a raid on the border. I had to tell the Haputian soldiers I was from their country, or I could have been killed."

"Ah, I see," said Quip softly. At least she didn't ask how I came to be so near the boarder. We were silent for a moment, and then she said, "You should come with us next time we go help out in a raid. We can probably send a few Laitmean soldiers your way to take you back to your own country." I hesitated before answering. Her offer was generous, to say the least, for it meant putting their own lives at risk, not to mention forfeiting the reward they would doubtless receive for turning me in. Especially if they found the book and realized what it was...

Fortunately, before I could answer, Trill spoke.

"Looks like we'll spend a night in the cellar after all," she remarked.

"What?" I asked, horrified.

"Redge keeps count of who comes down early through the cracks in the floorboards," Quip explained. I looked up at the ceiling, where there were several large cracks in what would be the floor of the boys' dormitory.

"Oh, dear," I sighed. This day was getting worse and worse. "At least Redge won't be down there with us." But the moment I spoke, I knew I had made a mistake. Trill and Quip grinned at each other.

"Who says he won't be?" asked Quip. I groaned. Somehow, I know Redge will be down there with us tonight. Along with all the spiders, mice, and other nasty creatures that live there.

Well, I suppose I ought to stop writing for now. It is getting dark and directly after dinner, we four shall be locked down in that dungeon for the night. How will I survive? I'll be alone, in the dark, with a cruel boy eager to beat people and two girls who know I am their enemy and carry knives and truncheons! Why, oh why, did I leave Laitmea? I'm beginning to think even servitude could not be as bad as this!

The Warrior

Year 111, 28th day of spring

Boy, is that new girl trouble. She got us all in the cellar. Her, Redge, Trill, and my ownself, that is. Her name's Ettalara. I'll have to come up with some suitable insults. Says she's Laitmean. Trill thinks we should help her out just to get rid of her, but I wonder if we could lead her towards the border and then double cross 'er and have some friends from the Haputian army waitin. That'd serve her right, wish there were more of them around for me to trick. Laitmeans. The scum. LAITMEA IS BAD. THEY HAVE NO RIGHT TO TAKE OUR LAND, OR MAKE US PAY TRIBUTE. HAPUTA FOREVER!!!!!! Alright, on to business. If I ever get the plague again, I'll go to Laitmea and see how many people I can infect before I die. My parents died of it, they can too. Trill just hit Redge. The new girl, sorry, ETTALARA, is insulting our clothes. Thank you, Ettalara, least I'm not dressed like you. I swear I will feed her to a dragon. TOES FIRST. SLOWLY. But first I'll steal her sewing needle, pick the lock to the sewer gate, and go kill some Laitmean scum with Trill. Let's hope the new girl doesn't try to tell on us. I'll find a dragon all the faster if she does.

Redgenold

28th of spring, year 111

    The cellar again. I dare say that this is a new record. I saw the girls go down early, and let the matron know that it was Quip, Trill, and Ettalara- the new girl- who had woken her. I mainly do this so that matron isn't cruel to me, for as I mentioned before, she did not approve of my mother. Quip does not understand this, however, and so took the soonest opportunity to fight me. I rose to her bait, foolishly, it turned out, but I can't help it when she looks at me with those big green eyes. When we were caught, as Quip knew we would be, I was sentenced to share the cellar with the three girls. I watched Quip from the corner of my eye for a while, but Trill noticed, and clobbered me. I was only out for a second, but when I came to, my head hurt, so I lay still. Quip and Ettalara were having an argument, which I gathered was about a sewing needle. When I heard footsteps receding, I understood. There is a tunnel out of the cellar, which I doubt the matron knows about, but it is locked up anyway. Quip took the needle to pick the lock so she could join the skirmish I heard starting. After a moment, my head felt a little clearer, so I began to sit up, then I heard a gasp and more footsteps- Ettalara was bolting out the passage. Imagine! She's more afraid of me than Quip and a battle! I got out this book, and was filling it out in the predawn light filtering in from the passage, when I heard the most frightful noises coming down from above. Laitmean soldiers will often chase Haputian raiding parties through the streets if the Haputians get too bold- it invariably happens when Quip goes out with the men- some think we shouldn't go after the Laitmean border guards at all, but they don't dare say so when the girls join a raid. I usually just jam my head under a blanket and go back to sleep when the clamor dies down- but this was different. There were more boots tramping on the street, and more shouts and screams than there ever have been before. It sounded more like the raiders were fending for their lives than evading a small group of guards. I kept my ears pricked, listening for Quip's return, until a few minutes ago, when I heard an unbelievably loud bang. The noise of it shook the dust from the rafters, and scared me half to death. I do hope that it's shaken the lock on the door to the stairs out of place, for I don't want to be in the cellar if this building comes down.

12

135 For the love of gunpowder.
Oh lily white dust
for which men lust.
It is expedient
that we have this ingredient
to add to our unholy mix.
A sea-man from Mer had some on his hands,
for he sold it in distant lands.
His crew had a fire lit,
round it on cold nights they would sit.
'till their captain was blown to the moon.
Oh, black powder,
make the noise louder!
Gone with a bang
the arrow that sang.
Here to stay a more devilish weapon.
Now the battle is won
by a thing called a gun.
Though as oft as it fires,
its owner expires.
As for its larger counterpart-

Stay back when they light the fuse,
unless you wish to lose
a hat, a shoe,
a limb or two,
perhaps your life.
Yes a cannon's a mighty fine thing,
for death and destruction to bring.
Alike on friend and foe
quite a lot of woe.
All for the love of gunpowder.

The Warrior

Year 111, 29th day of spring

The Laitmeans are defendin' their borders with cannons now. Or tryin' to. Last night one of them exploded, and Trill got hit in the shoulder by a fragment of the casing. Well, that's how it goes with things what go boom. Either they don't go boom at all, and you're fightin' useless metal stick against our good old sharp implements, or they explode in a big way and destroy the one that was firin' them along with the one that was bein' fired at. Either way, Trill's shoulder doesn't look too good. Ettalara was following us, and she acted like she's never seen blood before. I made her help with dragging Trill, and now we're back in the cellar. Trill is sleeping now, and Ettalara is sitting and moping. I should probably just kill her now, but my leg's hurt. I don't need any help, but I'm not in any condition to fight. Which is no good, because Laitmea is full on invading. With my bum leg and Trill's banged up shoulder, we're sunk. I reckon Ettalara will be back with her own folks soon. DEATH TO LAITMEA, HAPUTA FOREVER!!!

Redgenold

30th of spring, year 111

The whole city has been overrun, and all of us orphans carted off as slaves. I ran the stairs two at a time after the bang- I heard that it was a cannon, a giant firecracker, or a dragon. I presume it was not a dragon. All the little ones were crowding down to the matron's room, wailing and frightened when the Laitmean soldiers broke down the door and ordered the lot of us out. I breathed a sigh of relief that Quip had run off- too soon. They dragged her, Trill, and Ettalara up from the cellar a moment later. Trill was nursing a bandaged shoulder and still unsteady on her feet, though Ettalara seemed unscathed. Quip was limping something terrible and spreading blood over the floor, but when a man tried to pick her up, she punched him in the gut. I tried to end up beside her in the wagons we were pushed into, but instead, I was plunked next to the horse driver. We were bumped and rattled along for what must have been more than a day, though I dozed off for a while and cannot say for sure. We were then jammed into what can only be called cells, two or three in each, which are so small as to make the orphanage seem a paradise.

The Warrior

Year 111, 30th day of spring

   Laitmeans got us. Reckon they're gonna train us for slaves. Funny thing is, Ettalara never said a thing. I bet she's just a coward, and doesn't want to speak up, just like a typical Laitmean. She'll go back to her people soon enough; somebody's bound to notice that she's not Haputian. Wonder how she likes hard labor. Finally a Laitmean gets a taste of real work! It'll do her good. She spent the whole wagon ride here in a fit o' sullenness. Guess it must be pretty bad to be her. Taken prisoner by her own people. Serves her right. Trill is a little better now, but my leg is worse. I hope it gets infected. If I get weak enough the Plague will come back, and I can give Laitmea what it deserves. DEATH. Right now I think the slave drivers are just trying to break us. Ha! I will not break! I will give them all plague and then find a dragon and teach it to eat people I don't like. Trill says much the same. Haputa forever. Maybe we should light something on fire. I think that's on the list.

The Lady

~❦~

31st Day of Spring

What a remarkable turn of events. I am now a captive of my own people. This is of course *not* my fault, as Quip seems to think. I have not told the soldiers who I am, but *not* because I am a coward, which is also what Quip seems to think.

We were all down in the damp, dark, and dreary cellar, but not all of us were awake, as Trill had already knocked Redge out with her truncheon. We could hear sounds of another skirmish above, and shortly after Redge was knocked out, Quip and Trill decided to go up and fight. I thought then that they were crazy. Correction, I *knew* then that they were crazy.

"How do you plan to get out?" I asked, "In case you haven't noticed, we are locked in." Quip looked annoyed.

"There's another entrance," she said.

"Is it just... open?" I asked, confused. It wasn't much of a punishment if the children could get out so easily.

"No, of course not! It's locked like any other door in this place."

"Oh." Suddenly, Quip got a thoughtful look on her face.

"You sew, right?"

"Yes..."

"Do you have a needle?"

"Yes..." Quip held out her hand expectantly. I wanted to refuse (especially

47

because she stood there, so confident I wouldn't) but then I remembered that she and Trill had weapons and I did not. I decided I would need to get myself a fencing foil as soon as possible. But for now, there was nothing to do but hand it over. I did so with a sigh.

"You stay right here, and we'll send some soldiers down to fetch you," Quip called as she and Trill disappeared into the darkness. I sat down, exasperated. Quickly, I stood up again. Redge was stirring! I was not about to be trapped down there with Redge for my only companion! I would emerge in the morning black and blue! So, against my better judgment, I hurried off in the direction of Quip and Trill.

This time, Quip looked exasperated.

"What are you doing here?" she hissed.

"Guess who woke up?" I replied. Quip sighed.

"Alright, you can come, but stay behind us and away from the battle." They finished picking the lock and we all ran out into the night.

I climbed a tree a fair distance from the battle as Quip and Trill rushed to join it. I pulled out my little knife. It would not do much good in a real fight, but it was better than nothing. I searched for the girls, but could only see Trill. She wielded her truncheon quite skillfully; all who opposed her fell or fled. I soon lost sight of her, as the battle raged on.

The Laitmeans seemed to be losing badly. They didn't even seem to be trying! When all seemed lost for them, the soldiers suddenly broke formation to allow something to pass between them. A cannon! I had heard of these things, but never seen one before. It is the most powerful weapon yet. (Well, besides a dragon, but as far as I know no one has ever succeeded in training one of those and would have to be insane to try.)

I quickly got down from the tree, and moved away from it, lest it fall in the blast. I tried to shout a warning to Quip and Trill, but I could not see either. Suddenly, the loudest explosion I have ever heard rang out and was followed by a cloud of dust. I dropped to the ground, covering my head as debris rained down upon me. As soon as it was over, I jumped up and ran into the thick of the confusion, looking for the girls.

And then I saw Quip, leaning over Trill. She was dragging her out of the fray, but not making much progress. I ran up and lifted Trill's legs as Quip held her under the arms and together we brought her just past the edge of the battle. By now, most of the Haputians were fleeing the scene, and while I was glad for the victory of my country, I wondered what it meant for us.

We lay Trill down as gently as we could upon the grass and I realized her shoulder was bleeding.

"She was hit by a canon fragment," Quip explained. Trill was not crying, but I could tell she was in a great deal of pain. I took out my handkerchief and tied it securely around the wound.

"We need to get her out of here," said I, glancing about anxiously, "She needs proper medical care."

"I'll be fine," Trill groaned through gritted teeth.

"We should take her back to the orphanage," I argued.

"It will be overrun with those dirty Laitmean soldiers and the children will be taken as slaves." Quip snapped.

"Then where can we go?" I asked, trying not to sound as panicked as I felt..

"Back to the cellar," Quip replied, "I can't think of anywhere else, and they'll probably start to burn the city soon." We made our way back there and locked the door that led outside. I could hear shouts and loud thumps from up above. It sounded as though the soldiers were tearing the orphanage apart!

We had been sitting there for several minutes when the other door to the cellar opened and we heard voices drawing near.

"They're coming down," Quip whispered.

"Isn't there anything we can do?" I asked. I couldn't be captured, not now! If the soldiers found me with the book, they would assume I had stolen it and I could be killed on the spot!

"If we go back into the open, we'll be captured anyway. We may as well stay here," Quip replied as the voices got even louder and a torch came into view. "Brace yourselves. Here they come."

The soldiers hurried us outside where we were searched. I hid my book in my dress, but they took my bag. Quip and Trill hid their weapons, too. They threw us into a dark wagon with bars on the windows to prevent escape. I caught myself and stood upright, but Trill tripped coming in and Quip landed on top of her. The soldiers slammed the door and a moment later we lurched forward, off to who knows where. Quip says we will be trained as slaves. Disgraceful! I can't believe I, a girl of noble birth, could become a slave. I must not let it happen! I'll escape, or... Someone is coming!

The Thief

31st day of spring

Wow! So much has happened since I last wrote! But wait, I'll start from the beginning…

So Quip and I, talked together quietly. We knew Ettalara had seen us when we helped in a raid a few nights after she arrived. And we knew she couldn't be from here because she was too grand.

As we were discussing this, Ettalara woke up. She yawned in a most unladylike manner.

"Did you see us last night?" Quip demanded.

"Yes," she replied without thinking. I sighed slightly. Silence. Then Quip asked,

"Where are you from?"

"Here," Lara said, shifting uncomfortably. (I'm calling her Lara now, don't know if she approves.) Quip tried questioning her further, but she stood stiffly.

"I'm going down to breakfast," she announced. I shook my head dumbstruck. Didn't this girl know you could get in trouble for going downstairs too early? Quip glanced at me and we both followed, though we knew we'd be put in the cellar for sure. (I didn't mind, though. Unlike the other orphans, I look forward to the cool passages and the long, mysterious tunnels.) We sat down on the bench next to Lara.

"You're from Laitmea, aren't you?" Quip demanded. Lara pulled her knees up to her chest and did an eye roll, (one I'd see very frequently in the coming days).

"Yes," she admitted, sullenly, "I was trapped in a raid when I wandered too far. I had to tell the raiders I was one of them or they'd have taken me prisoner."

Quip's composure at Lara's confession was amazing. To learn that she was our enemy was pretty blood chilling to me. Oops! Quip is calling me for dinner. Write more later.

Redgenold

32nd of spring, year 111

Slavers take children often, so we've all heard of the horrors we'd face if we were bad, but listening to matron snap at us about it and living through it are two different things. I worry for Quip- she's a strong personality, and the slave drivers don't like that. They'll have to beat her within an inch of her life to break her- if she'll break at all. She might just snap and kill us all in our sleep. As for me, I fear the whip.

The Lady

32nd day of spring

   That was the guard. We were escorted outside to begin our training, mostly lifting heavy things. Now my hands are all cut and bleeding, my fingers are stiff, and I broke a finger nail. After the training, we were brought here to this dirty and completely unhygienic jail cell.

   The only thing that makes me persevere and keeps me from revealing my identity to the soldiers is the book. I must not, cannot let my mother and my country down. If I thought these soldiers would recognize me, I would explain my plight, but they would most likely assume I was lying.

   And to think this day is my birthday, too! I turned fifteen today (at 10:43 in the morning to be exact) and nobody knows or cares! At my last birthday celebration, my parents threw me a wonderful party. There was a feast in the grand dining room (we had another dining room for everyday). My friends came, and there was dancing and games and gifts! My sixteenth birthday was to be a much grander occasion, as sixteen marks becoming a woman and being introduced to society. On that day, I was to have a lavish party with hundreds of wealthy nobles and their families. The party would last all day and there would be horse races and competitions and lots of wonderful food and an elaborate ball with everyone in new ball gowns to top it all off. It is not uncommon for the royal family to make an appearance, either. Now I do not know if I shall even live to be sixteen.

Redgenold

36th of spring, year 111

My hands hurt too much to write of anything. Even Quip.

The Thief

38th day of spring

I'm back! I don't have much time, so I'm going to summarize some things.

Redge spied on us through the cracks in the floorboards that morning we talked to Lara, so we did get put in the cellar. Somehow, Quip arranged it so that he was in there too. To torture Ettalara, maybe.

Anyway, we left the cellar by using the passage when we heard there was a raid going on above us. We joined in. The battle was incredibly large for just a skirmish but we didn't complain or back down, just charged into it. Unfortunately, we missed that the Laitmeans had a cannon that they were eager to test. Cannons are very dangerous, and prone to falling apart, which this one did in dramatic fashion, killing everyone who was too near it. When it exploded, I was hit by a cannon fragment in the shoulder and Quip and Lara were forced to carry me back to the passage, but soon, the Laitmean soldiers found us. Why Lara didn't say she was one of them I don't know, but then we were taken prisoner and taken to be trained as slaves. This is where I am now.

3

16 Just Desserts?
When kept in a prison, recall,
If you've done nothing wrong at all,
You lack of treason
Is all the more reason
For your captors to cause you to fall.

The Warrior

Year 111, 46th day of spring

They decided to whip Trill and me 'cause we didn't behave. Something about having to bring the soldier the rock when he asks. I'm stuck in a dark room with Trill, in a bit of pain, and really cold. I think I'll read the list for comfort. I'd forgotten that I even had it. What a sweet surprise. I think Trill's got a thing to read too, not sure what.

Quip and Trill's List of

Rules That Must be Broken

and Ways to Break Them.

By Quip

1. Stealing is not allowed. We have stolen stuff. CHECK.

2. Hitting people is frowned upon. We beat Redge up (not without good reason). CHECK.

3. Lighting things on fire is fun. We need to do that.

4. We need to tame a dragon.

5. We need to become pirates.

6. Stabbing people is not a good idea. I've done that. CHECK.

7. We haven't been branded.

8. We just got whipped. Doin' good. CHECK.

9. We need to give Laitmea the plague

10. Once we're pirates, we need to throw someone overboard.

11. A) We really need to get a dragon, and
    . B) Feed Ettalara to said dragon.
    . C) and make her walk the plank.

Now I can sleep. It's nice to plot stuff, and it distracts me from the pain, and the Laitmean soldiers who need DEATH.

Redgenold

46th of spring, year 111

Quip has been whipped. I so want to comfort her, but she doesn't seem to want comforting. When I tried to sit near her at meal time, such as it is, she hit me, so subtly that no one knew why I doubled over.

The Thief

47th day of spring

My shoulder throbs, but I must tell you, I found a book in the little shed they locked us in. I glanced inside and saw it was Lara's. It has different numbers next to the side of the page. Code! I figured it out after they took Quip and I out to be whipped for disobedience (My back will never recover from the whipping). The book is full of poetry. Each poem has a number before the title. You must count the words of the poem and the word you land on is the code! I think the number above the title tells you the order the poems are to be read in, but I'm not sure. Soldiers are coming to get us. I have to go...

7

4 Thief!
A treasure was kept by a dragon
Who guarded his hoard in a wagon,
An ant did come in
And make off with a pin
And the beast then wept into a flagon.

The Lady

46th day of spring

Quip and Trill are still outside. I'm not sure why. I suppose now is a good time to get my book before they come back. We were given new dresses this morning before training, quite plain and ugly, and so I had to take the book out of my old dress and hide it in this room. I had almost forgotten about it until this moment, so I had best fetch it now.

THE BOOK IS GONE!!!!!!! I have searched this room from top to bottom and there is no sign of it! Did the guards find it? If so, why wasn't I summoned instead of Quip and Trill? I am so scared! WHAT HAPPENED TO IT???!!!

Quip and Trill! That's the only explanation! They must have taken it! If they don't have it when they come back in, I'll... Wait! Here they come!

* * *

48th Day of Spring

I was right! It was them! They stumbled into the room (I found out they had just been whipped, but I was much too angry to think about their discomfort.)

"All right, where is it?" I demanded, holding out my hand.

"Where's what?" Quip asked with a grimace, as she eased herself onto a bench.

"You know!"

63

"You mean this?" Quip pulled out the book and passed it to Trill. I tried to snatch it from her, but Trill held it away from me and began to thumb through it.

"Give it back!" I hissed.

"This is strange," Trill remarked, "There are numbers on the pages, but they don't match up." Then her face cleared, "Oh, I bet you have to count the number of words on each page to spell out a message."

"Stop it! That's mine! Just give it back!" I would have tried to grab it again, but by this time Quip had pulled out her knife and was inspecting it, while watching me out of the corner of her eye, so I decided it would be foolish to attempt it.

Trill had been going along just fine, much to my dismay (who knew an orphan girl could read so well?), until she got a few pages in.

"Huh, the number is three thousand nine hundred and ninety three, but there aren't three thousand nine hundred and ninety three words in the first poem."

"Try reading it backwards," Quip murmured. Trill counted.

"Nope, still doesn't make sense." Suddenly, her eyes brightened, "Wait, what if it's not three thousand nine hundred and ninety three, but thirty nine, ninety three?" She counted. "Yes, that could make sense!" She and Quip turned to me for confirmation, but I was not going to give in that easily.

Quip must have guessed this, because she skipped negotiation and went straight to force.

"Tell us," she demanded coolly, pointing the knife at me. I tried to edge away, but the blade followed, drawing nearer to me. I began to panic. Should I lie and say they were wrong? No, if they figured out I was deceiving them, who knew what they would do. I hated myself for giving in so easily, and I'm sure many others will judge me even more harshly for my lack of defiance, but I bet they'd change their tune if the knife was pointing at *their* neck.

"Yes, that's right," I said. Then, because they seemed to be waiting for something more, "I suppose you want me to read the rest?"

"If you don't mind," said Quip. Of course, I did mind, but it didn't look like my opinion was going to matter much. Trill held the book out to me and

I took it, briefly considering lying again, before dismissing the idea. They could just recount the words to know whether I had told the truth. So, I read the correct words all the way through, stopping when I reached the end.

"That is all," I said, looking Quip in the eye and hoping she would believe me. I couldn't afford to let her suspect there was anything else. She took the book from me and studied it closely, before handing it back to me. I really shouldn't write any more about our conversation. I don't want this journal to become an instruction manual to the book. Suffice it to say, I was much alarmed by what they had discovered and have determined to stick closely to them. Who knows what they will do with such information.

The Warrior

Year 111, 48th day of spring

Things just get stranger and stranger. This mornin' I woke up, and checked my leg. The infection is bad, but isn't really my biggest problem. Apparently that book Trill's got is Lara's. It's a little book of poems. Strange thing is, the numbers on the pages don't make sense. There's two numbers on some pages, and none on others, and sometimes they count up, and sometimes they count down. Trill reckons it's some sort of code, so she tried counting words. Y'know, if the number's eight, look at the eighth word of the poem. It seems to say something about treasure, or maybe a forest, but past the first few words we can't make anything of it. Ettalara was none too happy that we had it, but she didn't explain anything much but read the code words. So least I know that the top number says the order you read 'em, (cause they're all out of order, fifth and then first and what not) an the next says what word to count too. Go figure. I reckon Lara's no commoner, if I had to bet, I'd say this book is worth about as much as the senate meeting we overheard. Anyways, before I spend too much time writing, I should put this down, just 'cause. DEATH TO LAITMEA, HAPUTA FOREVER!

The Thief

48th day of Spring

Quip and I forced Lara to tell us the code. It is about treasure and weapons guarded in caves. No wonder she's been so secretive about her bag! If someone were to find that, Laitmea would be ruined and destroyed. Lara was going to give it to her king when she got caught in the raid. Apparently, it's the only copy. I'd better close these pages. Quip is ready to go to bed and Lara is glaring at whoever even moves. She's boiling mad. Well, bye!

The Warrior

Year 111, 49th day of spring

I've got the plague again. Too soon. I can make Laitmea suffer, but this is the end. There's no recoverin' from a second bout of plague. Trill doesn't know. I don't think she needs to. Ettalara seems overly concerned with my well-being. I think she is hopin' that I can help her escape. Maybe I will. Maybe I won't.

Unless… there might be a way, but I'll not write it down just now. Let's just say I won't admit defeat so soon. I think I will get Ettalara out of here, if that's what she wants. She can come with me and Trill. If that's not what she wants, we'll take her anyway. She needs watching, 'cause she's a dangerous girl. Reckon it'll be better for all concerned if she comes quietly. We're gonna' get out of here soon.

The Thief

49th day of spring

As Lara, Quip and I were discussing what to do, Quip decided to share her darkest secret. I had known about it for years, but dared not write it in here. Now that Lara knows, I will.

Quip, her parents, and her family all had the plague. They died, but Quip survived. However, the plague is still in her body. It could come back anytime, but particularly when she is weak or sick. It is also very contagious.

Warning: if anyone finds this diary, PUT IT BACK!!

* * *

50th day of spring

We're out! Out of the slavery wagon that is. Not out of danger quite yet. Quip and I came up with the idea that we could pretend we had the plague so we would get an opportunity to escape. You see, if we failed all their examinations, they would put us in the sick wagon to be taken out of camp. We could escape then! Sometimes I wish I had Quip's brains.

It worked, but I had to show symptoms, too, since I had been with her the longest. I pretended to have symptom # 1; numbness.

I was swinging from one of the ropes they'd hung up for training, when I pretended to lose all feeling in my right hand. I let it drop uselessly to my side.

Only hanging onto the rope with one hand was challenging. I fell and landed on my backside. If Quip hadn't been in so much pain from the training, she would have been laughing her guts up. Lara snickered a little, though.

My acting was good enough. The slave traders threw us all in the sick wagon and drove us out of camp. On the way, Quip pried up a board in the floor of the wagon and we all dropped out and ran. Free at last!

I have to stop now. Quip is stirring on our makeshift bed in one of the city's alleys we walked to. I think she would tease me if she saw me with this.

Redgenold

50th day of spring, year 111

The plague wagon. I saw them take her away, her and Trill and Ettalara. It is a brutal illness, and if it has struck her again, there is little chance of her surviving. Still, she is strong, and may yet live. Sometimes the disease renders limbs useless, or destroys vision or sense of touch. It took the feeling in Quip's mouth, I know, which is why her smile is lopsided. I would hate for her to suffer blindness or worse. There are others- children mostly, who have been taken away for plague, and I fear that I may join them. Oh, Quip-

The Warrior

Year 111, 51st day of spring

I almost can't believe it worked. That Ettalara came with, that is. Of course the plan worked; I came up with it. I must say, jumpin out of a moving wagon was fun. I'm addin' that to the list. Tomorrow we'll reach one of the big cities. I've never seen so much wealth. Ha! I know where that comes from: Laitmea. Well, tough luck. Soon you won't be bossing Haputa 'round any more. Why, do you ask? Oh no reason, just a little thing called plague.

(and some top secret plans, AND we have Miss Ettalara, and will soon get some answers out of her.)

Anyway, DEATH TO LAITMEA!!!!!

The Lady

51st day of spring

We are finally out of that prison, thanks to Quip. I don't like her much, but I must admit, she did come up with a half decent plan. It worked, anyway.

First, we all had to pretend to have the plague. Quip, apparently, has had it before, and although Trill has known for some time, this was the first I'd heard of it. Now that I have been exposed, I, or Trill could come down with it at any moment. It is rather alarming, especially considering the fact that most people don't survive it the first time.

Anyway, we all had to show symptoms which include dizziness and impaired vision among other things. The less said about this adventure the better. The point is it worked and we all were put in the wagon with our belongings. As we were driving, Quip used her knife to pry open the floor of the wagon and we all dropped out of it. There were fewer guards than when we had arrived because no one wanted to be infected.

We made our escape successfully. We are now on our way to the pirates. For some reason, Quip and Trill wish to join them! Why I can't imagine, unless it is just to rob Laitmean ships. They would do just about anything to get revenge on my country. That is why I am coming along; to keep an eye on them.

Redgenold

51st of spring, year 111

The pins and needles numbness has started 'twixt my shoulder blades- I know that is how it begins, the tingling, all plague survivors say it, but I try to ignore it. Quip has not returned.

* * *

52nd of spring, year 111

I must have caught it when they passed around the water jug to all the children- one sip was all I took. My head throbs terribly, and my forehead is hot as the sun. My hands are numb as with cold, and my ears are ringing. At the least I should see Quip again before I die. If only I knew the words to tell her how I feel- horrible at the moment, but I mean how I feel about her, which is always well. Perhaps if all else fails I can give her a page from this diary.

* * *

53rd of spring, year 111

She is not here.

2

100 Upon the Sea
Beneath a sky of azure blue
lies an island, I tell you true.
Never cloudy is the sky, always warm the breeze,
always warm the sultry sun upon the boundless seas.
Never is there sorrow there, no never tears.
Ever is its beauty, ever are its years.
In state it lies upon the waves,
in beauty spends its endless days.
Peaceful, calm, apart it lies,
under clear and cloudless skies.
Lonely is the little place,
pinpoint prick in life's long race.
So far away from paths well trod,
though to it, desperate, we all plod.
What bounty lies upon its shores!
What treasure, truly all is yours.
This soft and pretty land,
to all belong its sands.
Though those who try to speed their coming never find its rest.
And kind it is to those who love it best.

What is this place, you ask with every breath?
In truth, this place is death.

QUIPENEAY

The Lady

53rd day of spring

I am exhausted! We've been walking for two days now with little food and water and no decent places to sleep. My dress is torn and dirty, my feet are sore, I am hungry and tired and stiff from sleeping on the ground and quite put out with Quip and Trill for deciding to find pirates in the first place!

* * *

58th day of spring (I think)

We have arrived in a town called Firdell. It's a small Laitmean about twenty five miles from the training camp, and close to my old home. Trill stole some food and Quip found a water supply. I'm a little suspicious at how eager she was to find water for us, but I don't suppose she could have done any harm. It's only water, after all.

The Warrior

Year 111, 58th day of spring

So now Laitmea has the plague. I spit in the main well, and lucky for them, I know that that's how it spreads. Trill got us some food, and now we're settin' off to become pirates. I hear that they have good medics. Maybe ones that can cure a second bout of plague. Anyway, being a pirate is on my list.

The Lady

60th day of spring

We have left Firdell and continued on our journey. I am beginning to grow used to life on the road, though I still don't enjoy it. We wake up at the crack of dawn every day, have a small bite to eat, and begin walking. We usually break for an hour or two in the afternoon when it is hottest. We use this time to eat whatever we can find and bathe or wash clothes when we come across a stream. Otherwise we sleep. Then we are on the move again and do not stop until the sun has nearly disappeared. We build a fire if it is safe, eat, and gather food for the next day (assuming there's any to be found) and then we all sleep. Speaking of sleep, I'm exhausted, so I think that's what I'll do right now.

Redgenold

60th of spring, year 111

I feel I should give an account of what transpired. I was taken to a building some miles into the countryside where they house the ill, and bury the dead. I looked in vain for Quip, until I called her name, and a man said, "There is no Quip here." She has died. I knew there was little hope of her recovery, but I had hoped. I fell so ill then that I could not write. My fever ran so hot I burned the children who touched me, and shook like a leaf in the wind. I remember little save my wish to die, but death refused to come. After a while, my temperature went down, and I began to recover. They give us no care at the sick house, only food if we can still eat. I starved myself for a while, but when the attendant saw that I was only grief sick and not ill, I was taken away and made to eat. Those that survive are still fit for slaves, and by then I was more than broken. I'll do their work if it kills me. I hope that it does.

The Warrior

Year 111, 61st day of spring

Walking to Mer would have been fun if Ettalara wasn't here. I swear I will feed her to a dragon, if ever I find one. They say I survived plague the first time because I was strong. I'll need that strength times ten, but Ettalara is sapping my will to live. LAITMEAN FILTH.

Redgenold

62nd of spring, year 111

I've been taken to row Laitmea's ships.

1

13 Irony
It's a thing that no one understands,
And yet it's known throughout the land.
It's more than just misfortune,
Irony's a double portion.
The knacker man can't find a ride,
Because his horse has sadly died.

The Lady

I have no idea what day of spring it is.

It rained last night, so we are all soaked to the bone. We haven't had food since yesterday morning and I'm so sore from walking I don't think I can take another step. If I weren't so certain Quip and Trill are up to something, I would have quit long ago and returned home.

The Warrior

Year 111, 67th day of spring

Oh what fresh hell is this? I feel myself growing sicker by the mile, and all Lara can think of is her princess life at home, that as far as I can gather she VOLUNTARILY LEFT? I try to hide how much I'm hurting, but it's hard when everything is in agony and I'm running a fever hot enough to boil. Every step aggravates the cut on my leg that's a festering mess a day away from attracting maggots, and all because of those Laitmeans, ABSOLUTE SCUM THAT THEY ARE.

That's all.

9

47 In the woods I stand.
In bright woods I stand,
beneath green spreading trees,
and think of one who is not here,
nor ever shall be near
to me again.
Though warm the shining sunlight be,
cold the heart of tree,
and cold my heart,
since she sailed away.
In the forest I stand alone,
in this copse I weep.
Ever through the night I my vigil keep.
Let my return to her come soon.

Redgenold

75th of spring, year 111

I do not cry for Quip anymore, but there is an ache in my chest that has naught to do with pulling on oars all day.

The Warrior

Year 111, 75th day of spring

I reckon that I'd better write some more. I've been feeling very light headed recently which is nice because it's hard to feel bad, but not nice when I forget what's been going on for the last hour. Trill might've noticed the last time I came close to falling, but hopefully she just put it down to my bad leg, which is still not much better. Trill's shoulder still ain't all the way mended either, and I reckon there's a piece of cannon still in there that we never got out, but it won't hurt her too bad. I only hope we get to where we're going before I drop dead. And speaking of our destination, everyone knows that outcasts and rebels go to Mer and join the pirates. That suits me, but not miss fancy pants complainer Ettalara.

'Oh, my dress is in tatters!'

'Oh, I'm cold.'

'Oh, this place is too dirty.'

'Oh, I don't want to be a pirate.'

As Trill would say, tough luck. I don't know who you are, or what your story is, but you come from Laitmea, and that's enough. You could have left, but you didn't, so now you are our hostage, or something very like it. LIVE WITH IT.

The Lady

I still don't know what day it is

Quip and Trill are whispering mysteriously on the other side of the fire and they won't let me join their conversation, so I decided to write. Not that there's much to record. What I wouldn't give for a proper bath, a decent meal, and a nice warm bed!

The Warrior

Year 111, 82nd day of spring

That medic had better be good.

Redgenold

84th of spring, year 111

   I will ever regret not telling her of my love whilst I still could.

The Lady

Three days from my last entry

Quip says we are nearing the pirate encampment and shall arrive there in less than five days time. According to Quip, there will be some sort of initiation before we will be permitted to join the pirates. When I asked what kind of initiation, Quip shrugged and said it would probably be some sort of fight as all pirates need to be able to fend for themselves in battle. Although I tried to act nonchalant when Quip told me this, I am very nervous. The only weapon I know how to wield is a fencing foil, and I have not had any practice in nearly a year. I then made the mistake of asking what happens to people who don't pass the initiation.

"They probably get thrown overboard," Quip replied.

"Or stabbed to death with a sword," Trill put in.

"Or fed to a dragon," Quip added with a grin. I shivered inwardly. Quip has made it no secret that that is what she would love to do to me. I know she and Trill are just waiting for me to fail. Well I won't give them that satisfaction. I can be a pirate if I set my mind to it!

The Warrior

Year 111, 90th day of spring
   Whoops, I almost missed a week, and I'll be missing a lot more than a week soon, my hands are barely still enough to write, and I think Trill must know somethings wrong that I'm shaking this bad.

* * *

Year 111, 1st day of summer
   So these are pirates. I like them. Unfortunately, you have to fight your way in. Unfortunate for Ettalara, that is. I wonder how fast she'll lose? I can't wait!!!
   I can't seem to clear my head, and this is rather hard to write, so I'll stop for now.

The Thief

2nd day of summer

Quip is not doing so well. Her face is flushed and she shivers even when it's not cold. She's almost fallen a number of times on our trip, too. I think the plague might have come back. It wouldn't surprise me, anyway, because her leg looks so infected I almost wonder if it should be amputated.

One the bright side, I have good news: I am a pirate! Don't believe me? Well listen to this…

After escaping, Quip said she knew where we were going, but I didn't expect her to go to the pirates of Mer! She told me we could rob Laitmea's ships. Sounded good to me, but not to Lara. She complained the whole time we were walking.

Once we got there, Quip demanded to see their leader, so a pirate showed us to their 'king'. He was tall, muscular, and would have been handsome if he didn't have a scar running through his cheek.

Quip explained that we wanted to join them and, I'm afraid to say, was quite rude and acted a little too full of herself. Lara later told me that she thought we'd be killed on the spot.

Lucky for us, however, the king of the pirates liked Quip at once and declared we'd all have to prove ourselves by fighting one of his henchmen in a duel. Because the king liked Quip, he fought her himself.

Quip's fight was sooo long, the pirates all called for them to stop and it ended in a draw. Lara's was shocking. She took a foil from the rack and met her opponent, who was slender and wielded a rapier. I hated the smirk on his face when he saw her, and I thought for sure she was finished. But instead, she dodged his blows easily and literally danced all around him. She gave a sudden thrust and he fell down with a good solid thunk.

I faced my opponent after she fought. He was tall and strapping. He held a morning star and swung it around his head like a rope. I whipped out my truncheon, and noticed the curve of its blade gleamed especially wickedly that day. Crouching, I waited. He whipped the morning star down and I rolled out of the way, a piece of my skirt ripping in the process. I stood and lunged for his neck, but he ducked and swung his weapon to his right, where I was. I leaned back far, farther, farther, and the spiked ball passed inches from my chest. He swore and tried to bring it down on my head. I circled around him, and in one leap, brought the handle of my truncheon down on his head. He fell and I ducked as his morning star descended also. I had won!

* * *

Later

"In here!" a pirate led Quip and me into a room where another man stood, holding a glowing iron stick.

No! I thought, *not this!*

He did Quip first. Hot tears ran down her face, but she didn't yell. I had never beheld such a scene. Quip never cried.

Then it was my turn. The pirate grabbed my arm and slammed it down on the table, pushing the hot iron rod into my flesh. Pain shot through me as it never had before and I couldn't help but cry out. Finally he pulled away and set the rod in its fire again. I glanced at my skin just below my wrist. It glowed red hot like the stick, but I knew that would fade. What wouldn't fade was the dagger that was now branded onto my skin for life.

The Warrior

Year 111, 2nd day of summer

That was fun. The person Trill was fighting made the mistake of pausing to flex his muscles and look intimidating. I think most people wait for him to strike first. That's why most people aren't pirates. Trill took him out in the first five minutes. I got stuck facing the leader of this band of curs. Lucky for me, I was allowed to pick any weapon to fight with and they gave me a set of daggers. I didn't know if I'd hold up so well, but I've been feelin' a little better. Or maybe much worse, I really can't tell if the salt air of the sea has done me good or if I collapsed a few days ago and had a really bizarre dream in my delirium. Given what happened with the little princess, I'm inclined to think the latter. Ettalara picked up this wimpy little sword, but managed to knock the other guy senseless. I knew she was more dangerous than she looked, but I did not expect that. Not the little princess after all, are you, Ettalara?

Redgenold

3rd of summer, year 111

Some of the slaves speak of revolt. I speak of nothing at all. What is there to speak of? My heart aches, my mind is naught but memories of Quip.

The Thief

3rd day of summer

When I woke in the cabin the pirates had given us, I immediately remembered the branding and looked at my arm.

"What do you think?" Quip broke into my thoughts. I blinked back tears and forced a smile.

"Great," I said cheerfully. Honestly, I'm a better actress than anyone thinks, because while on the outside I was calm and collected, inside, my thoughts were in turmoil.

All this! I thought angrily. *I've had to go through all this when all I really want to be is a dragon trainer!* There! I've said it! My secret that no one knows, not Lara, not Quip, not even my poor dead mother. I know it's practically impossible to be a dragon rider. That's why I've never told anyone. The dragon has to take a liking to you and you alone. Once you get one, you can fight with him and better yet, ride him! Just think! Soaring through the air with no cares in the world! There are only five riders in all of Eretz. All are men and all are experienced. I know if I told anybody about this, they'd laugh. But I know I could do it. Someday, I'll prove them all wrong.

* * *

Later

100

We found out later that Lara had chosen to work in the kitchens. She always comes to bed smelling like the horrid hot mush we are given for breakfast. Because she works in the kitchens, she doesn't have to get branded. I must stop writing, it's dinner time.

The Warrior

Year 111, 3rd day of summer

I've been branded a pirate! No going back now. Still feel alright, but a bit shaky.

5

76 Sail, if you like.
There are those who love the sea,
They sail the waves,
Boundless and free,
Far better than dry land's maze.
Some row ships of goods for trading,
Wealthy Lords sail for pleasure,
Pirates catch the winds for raiding,
Oh, the list goes on forever.
There are those who love the sea,
For whatever reason,
But you can guess that they aren't me.
I had a bad boating season.
Sailing ships are fine,
For merchants and for kings,
But if you don't mind,
I'll stick to other things.

The Lady

5th day of summer

We have joined the pirates. We passed the initiation which was fighting a pirate with a weapon of your choice.

When we requested to join them, Quip got smart with the pirate king (why, I don't know, Quip seems to enjoy constantly putting her life in danger) and he demanded to fight her. It ended in a draw.

Trill fought a particularly tough looking pirate who didn't seem to expect her to last more than three seconds. However, he was the one who didn't last more than three seconds. Trill knocked him out with one swift blow.

I faced a very intimidating looking pirate. I wasn't sure I would win, but fortunately, I was so much smaller than he was that I dodged his blows easily, stabbed him in the arm, and eventually brought him to his knees. He wasn't very happy about that, though.

Quip and Trill joined the raiding group while I became a member of the kitchen crew. It consists of two girls a bit older than me and one pirate who never helps out, just watches from his position by the door. I guess it's to make sure we don't try to poison anyone. That idea has entered my mind, but I don't want to poison all the pirates, just a certain member of the raiding group.

I don't like the other kitchen girls much. They think they are smart, but they don't even know what marzipan is or how to properly set a table! At first, they tried to boss me around and make me do all the dirty jobs, like washing dishes or scrubbing floors. But they gave up on that when I threatened to get Trill to hit them with her truncheon. I'm not sure if she actually would, but the other girls fear Quip and Trill more than any of the other pirates, so my threat was effective.

The Thief

~❧❦❧~

6th day of summer

I still don't believe what happened.

But wait! I must start, as always, from the beginning. Last night, we saw a ship approaching. Immediately, the pirates got ready. Quip got up on the ropes and stared out toward the ship. I watch her. I wish I weren't so afraid of heights. Imagine! Me, the 'dragon rider' afraid of heights! I must conquer that fear. I gazed up at Quip, her short blonde hair flying out behind her. I couldn't help but grin as I remembered how her hair got so short.

You see, Quip had longer hair, but she grew tired of it, so Lara agreed to cut it with her knife. However, I opened the door to the cabin we're in, and it bumped into a chair which fell down on top of Lara, so the perfect cut turned into a lopsided jagged edge. Lara tried to smooth it out, but Quip was stuck with bobbed hair. Lara was horrified and kept apologizing until Quip told her to shut up. I dunno, I think the haircut suits her.

Anyway, I watched Quip scale the ropes all the way to the Crow's Nest. She turned and beckoned me to join her. I shook my head and turned to go back down below deck. I glanced up one last time to see Quip laughing and talking to one of the pirates. Lucky. Quip get along with everyone! It's impossible to do something without Quip doing it better. Ugh, Trill, *Stop!* I must not be envious. I should get back story.

Ahem. There was a raid. (Isn't that a great start?) We boarded another ship and took all the treasure and prisoners we could find. When we got to the middle of the ship Quip handed me a torch.

"Go ahead," she grinned. I lit the ship on fire and took off like lightning. Soon, the ship was blazing all around me. Quip was already down in the rowboat yelling at me to hurry. I ran for the rope to climb down when a flame leaped out at me. I turned around and circled back, looking for someplace to get off.

I heard a scream and glanced back. The rowboat was heading back for our ship! Quip was screaming that I wasn't there. I had only one choice. Dive.

Fire all around me, I tried to make my way toward the side of the ship. A large barrel rolled and blocked my path.

"Blast!" I muttered. I looked everywhere until I saw one small opening, but the fire was quickly spreading.

"Now!" I yelled, (why I'll never know) and dove for it, toppling over the side of the boat. I screamed, flailing my arms and legs.

Uh oh. I don't know how to swim, was the thing that popped into my head as I plunged into the sea.

Then, I heard someone above me, paddling. Quip was coming. She pulled at my blue dress by the faded, wet collar, and hauled me back to the rowboat. Ropes pulled us up to the pirate ship, and Lara handed both of us blankets.

The pirates surrounded Quip, shoving me to the side to cheer for her. I forgot. Most had never seen someone risk their life for another. Only Lara stayed back, watching over me. Now she seemed like my mother. She put her arm around me.

Suddenly I couldn't bear it any longer. I yanked away and raced down below. It was the first time I had let my emotions show since mother died. I found a secluded corner, plopped myself down, and cried. I cried about losing my mother, the only person who ever really cared for me. I cried about my envy of Quip. But most of all, I cried because I realized that if I can't handle this, how will I ever handle a dragon?

The Warrior

Year 111, 6th day of summer

Raids are fun. Who would have thought that stealing stuff and lighting ships on fire would pay so well?

* * *

Year 111, 7th day of summer

Today is my birthday. I'm fifteen. Practically of age! Well, if I've made it this far, I might as well live a while longer. Still going to get checked out by the medic though, and see what the chances of full recovery are, maybe get my leg tended to, cause it's started to scar all frightening lookin. I'd like to live to sixteen, so I'll actually be legally old enough to illegally jump on other peoples' ships. Which is what I'll do now. Legality. Ha!

The Lady

8th day of summer

Quip and Trill seem to love the life of a pirate. They're always swinging on the rigging or practicing their fighting skills, or raiding ships and burning them. I hope we don't have to stay here much longer. The pirates are a bad influence on the girls. (Actually, they're a bad influence on the pirates, come to think of it.)

The only good thing about being with the pirates is that we are getting three meals a day. They mostly consist of bread and porridge and soup, but it's better than nothing, I suppose. I like to think the food improved once I joined the kitchen.

Redgenold

8th of summer, year 111

If ever I could escape these chains, I don't doubt I'd throw myself overboard. I still think of her, dead of plague. When I row the ship, the manacles at my ankles chafe, giving me horrible sores.

* * *

9th of summer, year 111

SHE'S ALIVE! Oh, I am a happy man! The others think me knocked silly as I sit and laugh for joy-I can hardly believe it, but I'll give an account:

The Laitmean army requires large amounts of gunpowder for the newest experimental cannons. Our captain was tasked with shipping several casks of powder from the port at Arlif around the coast of Mer, and into Laitmea. The journey to Mer was six hundred leagues by sea, and I was rowing most of it, as the winds were foul. We meant to pass through the Bay of Dragons on our return, but were blown somewhat North of our intended course. We avoided a shipwreck on Death's Cliff Bluff, albeit barely, but the archipelago is prime territory for pirate attacks. Around noon the day after the storm, another ship drew near us, a small, sharp- prowed ship.

When the captain saw they were flying the black flag, he loosed out chains and had us row like mad. He didn't want to lose valuable slaves if the ship went down, so he set me to man the canoes we used to get to shore. We could put them down in a pinch. The shorter vessel caught us before we went two miles, though. Men tried to board us using hooks and ropes. They threw them up as fast as we could cut them down. The braver souls had climbed the mizzenmast of the pirate's vessel, and flung themselves onboard our deck from above. That was what she did. Most of our food supply had been taken, along with those slaves and seamen who had not gotten to the canoes. I was fending off a burly man with an ax; for fear of losing my life, not our cargo. Pirates have limited use for gunpowder, so much of our stores were not taken. I knew that when they lit the ship on fire, we would be blown to smithereens. There was one pirate with a torch ready- she looked familiar. She was small, but sturdy, with long caramel colored curls and a very ragged blue dress, still a bit too big for her. Trill! If she had escaped, then perhaps it was possible—I thought my heart would burst right then. Quip! She was roped to the mast of the pirate ship, when the mast leaned in, she let go, and sailed down, landing like a cat, with the second torch in her hands. Quipeneay! How she lived I may never know, I only count myself lucky that she did. My ax wielding opponent saw what was happening and swore. He grabbed me round the middle and jumped ship- down to the pirates' deck. "Cut her loose!" was the cry. Trill and Quip- Quip! cut the ropes that joined the ships, and the pirates set off. I heard the merchant's vessel explode, but didn't see it, as I'd already been bundled below decks with the other prisoners. She's alive! My dearest, dearest Quip.

The Thief

9th day of summer

I lit the next ship on fire also. Not much else to tell. Quip is highly respected. Whenever she walks past, someone will call out to her to help him do this or that. Lara has been eyeing me ever since yesterday. I try to avoid everybody.

Oh! I thought of something! While we were eating dinner, Quip said she saw Redge on board the ship we had just raided. Lara's spoon dropped at the news and I looked up sharply.

"I think he's in the dungeons," Quip said.

The ship rocked suddenly, which made me queasy. Redge on board! I'm not particularly afraid of him. Just of what he can do.

Blah! Rough night tonight, I feel a little sick. I think I'll stop writing and go lie down in my bunk.

The Warrior

Year 111, 9th day of summer

There is one small problem. Just one, aside from the fact that I'm still a bit ill, and might lose my leg to gangrene or die of plague whilst I'm weak and recovering and that is, Redge has been spotted. Yes, horrid, smelly, beats-up-little-kids Redge. Last we saw him, he was being beaten up by Laitmean slave drivers, so goodness knows how he got here. What's more, I think I saw the other pirates drag him on board. No matter. Today we set up camp, and Trill and I are off to catch a dragon. Did I forget about dragon catching in my delirium? Not so! For the pirate's cove is near enough to dragon territory as ever it could be. And luckily, they should have hatchlings about now, so we just have to find a nest. We reckon that there's one about a mile south of the pirates camp, we'll just have to wait a few days to raid it. And then what have we? A beast of monstrous proportions, a winged horse of a kind or it will be. Trill's too chicken to go after an adult, so we'll have to take a tiny one and wait a half a season or so for it to grow up. Oh, and it'll have scales and spit that catches fire. All that to spell DEATH TO LAITMEA!!! Ha Ha! And a lovely present for Ettalara, who detests dragons. (May she never know that they despise manflesh and rarely eat anything smaller than a deer.)

Perhaps if we find on small enough, it'll think we're its parents. Then it'd be easy to train it to eat-I mean *be nice* to Ettalara.

The Thief

10th day of summer

Still not much happening. Last night, as we lay in bed, the talk of food came up and Quip got a wonderful idea for annoying Lara.

"You know how good beetles are?" she began, glancing at me slyly. I grinned and joined in.

"How about locusts? If cooked right, they're delicious!"

"Oh, and spiders!"

"Or flies!"

"Or ticks!"

"*STOP!*" Lara yelled, putting her hands over her ears.

"Dragonflies?" Quip asked. Lara shivered. Apparently she was listening after all.

"Ladybugs?" I started again. Lara groaned. We kept this up till we ran out of bugs. Then we talked about the fleas and ticks in the mattresses. Well, good night. Don't let the bed bugs bite!

* * *

11th day of summer

I am soooo excited! We are finally going to get a dragon! Quip and I are determined to kidnap a dragon and tame it to fight for Haputa. First, I want

114

to ride it. Oops, best be off, Lara's calling softly from the deck.

The Warrior

꩜

Year 111, 12th day of summer

Last night I spoke with one of the medics. He says I'm pretty bad. Most of the pirates have had the plague at some point, so he wasn't worried about me infecting anyone, but he was really worried about my leg. He said that I had to take better care of myself If I want to live. He says I might survive, if I get plenty of sleep and don't strain myself. We'll see how things go. Anyway, we now have a dragon. Took a bit of a hike to find a nest, but the Archipelago of Doom is the one place in Eretz where they live in great numbers. Trill and I have named it (think it's he, not sure yet) Dart of Doom, or Dart, for short. Trill is watching him now, and Miss Ettalara is watching me. She knows I have the plague, but Trill doesn't. I hope to keep it that way, 'cause if Trill finds out she'll kill me. It's probably more humane that way, but I want to see what'll happen when the plague takes its course. Anyhow, Death to (you guessed it) LAITMEA!!!

* * *

Year 111, 13th day of spring

We're still away on a "Scouting mission" for dragon theft purposes. I taught Trill to swim today while Lara was making dinner. Did I mention she's our cook? The last time I taught anyone to swim was before the plague took my family. I feel odd about it, somehow. Like I've let them go, and I'll never get them back now, which is silly, 'caus they're dead as dead can be. Even my Pa.

15

42 The Hunt.
Fierce is the mighty beast,
upon our bodies he shall feast.
Ten men went out to slay him, only one returned.
The other nine, it could be said, had their lesson learned.
Whichever man is lagging
shall be food for the Dragon.
The monster is no doubt
ever so strong and stout.
He has taught us all to fear
His stomach grumbling as we draw near.
Eleven men went out, for battle each one yearned.
Of the lot, none returned.
Four their foe did eat on sight,
seven more he set alight.
Imagine then his delight,
when twenty men came to fight!
Imagine then the feast he had,
(though some find it rather sad).
The moral of this story, friend?
Unless you wish to meet your end,

15

let sleeping monsters lie.
I would prefer you not to die.

The Thief

13th day of summer

We did it! We got off the ship and snuck off into the murky forests of the island. Of course, we're not in Mer, the seaport. We're on a neighboring island that is filled with dragons. We slipped into the dense forest and searched for quite a while.

Finally we spotted a nest. Three dragons were sleeping in it. The mother was gone, for now. We snatched, that is, Quip snatched, the smallest one there and we all took off. Quip handed it to me and I glanced down into its face. *Wow!* I thought. *I can't believe I'm holding a dragon!*

After much discussion, we decided on a name for the dragon, Dart of Doom. We just call him Dart for short. We walked a long way and put Dart in a little ditch. He's sleeping and I'm guarding him. Better tuck you away, Quip's coming. She'd laugh if she saw me writing.

* * *

Later

I forgot to tell you this, with all the excitement about Dart, so I'll tell you now.

A day before we got Dart, we were camped out under a crude shelter Quip set up with some borrowed goods from the pirate ship (yes, they really were borrowed this time. We headed back to the ship two nights later).

I was nearly asleep when Quip stood. She moved about stealthily and I was suspicious. I pretended to be asleep when she glanced over. Lara wasn't asleep or even trying to pretend to be and asked Quip where she was going.

"Back to the pirate ship. The plague inside me is back. I gotta go to their doctor. If anyone can help me, he can." She slipped outside and added, "Don't tell Trill. I'll be back," and then, she was gone.

Why didn't she tell me? Then it dawned on me. Of course! We went to the pirates in the first place so Quip could be healed by their doctors (because they're known to be the most well-trained in the land), plus she knew the plague was striking her again, so that has to mean she's contagious and Lara and I are exposed!

I suppose I should be mad at her for not telling me, but really, I'm almost flattered. She must have really thought I'd be furious or want to murder her or something. It takes a lot to win that kind of respect from Quip. And I'm obviously not sick or anything. What with that and Dart, I'm in a charitable mood, so I'll let it slide. Officially not bringing up the plague again.

A NEST OF DRAGONS

Redgenold

18th of Summer, year 111

To die myself, when she is only just found- I can hardly write of it. No one knows how or why pirates take prisoners-save those of us who have been taken, and we'll not be telling. It's like this: pirates don't have slaves, per say, but when the ship is going down, coming with them is better than drowning. But to let a man go free who knows where the pirates are, and what they are planning, would be foolhardy at best. So that leaves two choices. Either you join the pirates, from envy or cowardice. (The latter group gets killed sooner or later anyway,) or you drown. For moral high ground, I suppose. The Captain, for I still think of him as Captain, though he's just as much a prisoner as the rest of us, said not one of us is to join up, else he haunt us from the grave. Sailors being such a superstitious lot, that's enough to have most all of them sign on to walk the plank. As for me- well, he hissed at me through the bars, "If you won't go overboard, I'll push you. Not one of my men will turn coat on Laitmea, so help me." So I'll jump-little good it will do me. I never learned to swim. There are no lakes in Quirton, and the river's not fit for a human, unless he's dead. The ocean will have my body, Quip my heart. I don't know where the rest of me belongs now.

The Warrior

Year 111, 19th day of summer

We were going to slip away from the pirates today and take our dragon to Haputa, but we stopped for a moment too long, because the prisoners from our last raid were walking the plank. Guess who landed by us?

I am stuck on a tiny boat with Ettalara, Trill, Redge, and a baby dragon. Yep. Fun!

Redgenold

21st of Summer, year 111

Blessed luck, or damned luck, I don't know which. Blessed, because I am alive, sound in body, and on solid, dry ground, Damned, as just after our meeting, Quip and I are once again apart. It seems that joining pirates was merely a ruse that she and Trill employed to snatch a dragon. Sent out as scouts with a cook, (That Ettalara girl, if you'd believe!) they had ample time to search the Bay of Dragons- an aptly named place. As they were successful in catching one, they had no further need to be pirates, and left, under the cover of a second scouting trip.

The Warrior

Year 111, 21st day of summer

We've rowed (Trill and I, that is) up to the mouth of the River Quir. We're gonna dump Ettalara in Laitmea as soon as possible, minus her book of "Poems" 'reckon it's got the location of Laitmea's treasury in it, so we'll take it to the senate. Last we heard, (20th day of spring to be exact) they were in Quirton, so we reckon they're in the capital now, since that's the only other Haputian city big enough to hide out in. So we get the book to them, and Laitmea gets, wellll, not death, but they'll send some loyalists to steal as much of their money as they can. No funds, no army. No army, no invading Haputa! HAPUTA FOREVER, DEATH TO LAITMEA!!!!!!!! Also, we dumped Redge on the nearest bit of land we came across, in Mer, I think, though we're all a bit discombobulated in terms of direction. Nothing but the clothes on his back. Vengeance!

Little Monster

What teeth, what claws,
What scales, what paws,
What ivory horns and jewel bright eyes.
Wings of vellum, breath of fire,
And the forked tongue of a liar,
And a sweet voice with which he cries.
Oh, little monster.

Redgenold

22nd of Summer, year 111

It seems I dozed off before my tale was finished. I do not pretend not to love my country, but sometimes, I think those girls take things too far. This dragon, for example. Surely, if they train it for the army, which is no doubt what they intend, it shall be terrifying indeed, but such fruits do not seem worth the dangers one must face to achieve them. But I digress. My purpose is to record my own story, not debate the aims of Haputa's war. To this end- As earlier mentioned, I was given no choice but to walk the plank. I cannot overstate the terror I felt as I stepped onto it. Second to love, fear, I think, is the strongest emotion. When I jumped, I thought to die. But I hit wood, not water. You see, the girls had just set off with their dragon, and had not gotten far from the ship's side, so my flailing carried me to the edge of their small vessel. Ettalara pulled me back so I did not fall in the water, though I wished it had been Quip. Then again, had it been her, I might well have gone the other way. So I tried to find some sleep on the boat's floor, but got little. I could feel the little dragon looking at me. I could not read much in those fierce orange eyes, but I think the little monster hates me. And so, it seems, does Quip. She does not wish me dead, or she could have left me to the sea, but at the first sight of the mainland, I was left to fend for myself. I suspect that Ettalara will suffer the same fate. What Quip and Trill do is only for Quip and Trill. At least Ettalara hates them back. I cannot bring myself to hate Quip - seeing her so close, asleep in the boat, so peaceful, I almost cried that I couldn't bring myself to kiss her. But if I did, I would be drowned for sure. Nevertheless, some part of my mind says it would be worth it.

The Warrior

Year 111, 29th day of summer

Ettalara is dumped. I reckon we've got to find the Senate soon, 'cause those stinkin' Laitmeans are sending their army in. It's all out war now! F. U. N. (that's short for "For the love of hapUta, do Not invade us!").

I wonder how long it will take for Ettalara to figure out that her book is missing.

***

Year 111, 31st day of summer

Who should Dart find this morning? Ettalara followed us. Who knows how she got across the river!

We stole a horse at Quirton and are riding to Archon, with the dragon on my head, (He likes Trill best, and I said she should hold him, but she's got to control the horse, who doesn't like dragons, and she says he likes my head, dunno if that's a compliment or an insult). Ettalara's been complaining all the while.

'Why did you get that accursed dragon?'

'Why do you need to find the senate?'

Doesn't she know that it's all top secret? Even Trill and I aren't supposed to know.

The Thief

35th day of summer

We are in Haputa! Oh, to be home is glorious, but I must explain. We spent days training the dragon after we left the pirates. Frankly, I was surprised we escaped so easily. We simply took a rowboat and rowed off under the pretense of a scouting mission. The only problem we encountered was Redge, who walked the plank right into our boat.

Quip and I had trained Dart well and he didn't make any noise. We left Redge on the first bit of dry land we encountered.

We dropped Lara off on a beach we hoped was Laitmea. But, unbeknownst to Lara, I had slipped her book out of her bag.

Quip rowed for a few hours more and then we parked on shore to sleep.

"Well, where is it?" I awoke to see Lara glaring down at us. She had found us.

"What?" I asked, attempting to look innocent (which is hard to do when you've just been rudely awakened from slumber).

"My book!" Lara shouted, stamping her foot impatiently.

"What book?" Quip asked, grinning. She loves to tease Lara, and so do I. Uh oh, Dart's coming over, hope he doesn't chew on my diary…

The Lady

45th day of summer

  I haven't written in a while, but here is a quick summary of the events which took place. We were with the pirates for several weeks, before Quip and Trill announced we were getting a dragon. I was none too enthusiastic about this idea, but I was curious, so I went along. After stealing a baby dragon (which they named Dart of Doom and call Dart for short), we finally left the pirates by taking a rowboat. (We also had to pick up Redge who had managed to get himself captured by pirates and was then forced to walk the plank. We dumped him at our earliest convenience.) Quip and Trill dropped me off in Laitmea, but they had secretly stolen my book. So, I had to track them down by hitching rides on farmers' wagons (which was not easy). They then refused to give me my book until I gave them information and even used it as a chew toy for the horrid dragon to get me to talk! When I finally told them some information (which may or may not have all been true) they gave me back the book, but it was covered in dragon slime and was absolutely disgusting. I swear those girls are the most infuriating humans to ever walk Eretz!

The Warrior

Year 111, 45th day of summer

Anyhow, we got some straight answers out of Ettalara by having Dart play fetch with the book. She's trying to get the book back to her king. We think he's trying to destroy all records of the treasury so that they can't fall into the wrong hands, A.K.A. the Haputian Senate, which is exactly where we'll take it. Did I mention that my leg is all healed up? Got a bit of a limp, but nothing too bad.

11

19 The Stars
What lovely gems gleam in the sky,
That dance and glimmer miles high
And watch as world passes by,
And watch as world passes by.

Redgenold

53rd (most likely) of Summer, year 111

I am in Laitmea now, that I know. I have followed the River Quir for many, many leagues without meeting another living soul, and only a few dead ones. I have not left its bank, for I know that without its water I would surely die, but it is not the best water. Sometimes it has made me violently ill, even when boiled. Then it is hard for me to move at all. For days I sat under an oak tree, wracked with cramps before I was able to move again. At least it felt like days. I do not rightly know how much time has passed.

* * *

54th (again, speculative) of Summer, year 111

'Quip'. I know now I say it in my sleep. I woke to the sound of it again last night.

I am now dangerously close to the border with Haputa. I've lived my whole life not more than fifty miles from it, but things have grown worse since I was taken away. I learned that after Quirton was taken by Laitmea, it was taken back. It has been captured and recaptured some five times since. The fighting is fierce on both sides. To try to cross back into Haputa would be suicide. Staying here would be suicide.

* * *

55th (I shall keep this order of dates until I learn otherwise) of summer, year
111

    There was a skirmish last night. The Haputians came charging up a little
hill held by the local troop, and were cut down like grass. One of the men had
a gun. The things are hardly any safer than cannons, and sometimes kill their
owners, but even a shoddy one can do a lot of damage. A stray bullet grazed
my cheek as I watched from a distance. The cut stings a little and has started
to heal all ragged- It'll scar badly, I fear. I cut my hair with an abandoned
dagger this morning. It feels better to have it short again, the long strands
were tangled so badly no combing would have sufficed. About the hair on
my face I can do nothing- One slashed cheek is enough for now. I'll try to
find a mirror to clean myself up properly, but I'm a bit afraid of what I'll see.

The Warrior

Year 111, 55th day of summer

The dragon grows fast. He's gone from my head to my lap to running beside us since I last wrote, and he's stopped catching squirrels and moved up to beavers. Lara is disgusted. Laitmean sissy. Nothing else to report. Travel is quicker with a horse. Shame we didn't have on on the way to Mer, but one can't go stealing horses in Laitmea. They all belong to snobby rich lords over there, so you're killed if you take so much as a broken down old mare. In Quirton you only get a night and a day in the stocks for horse theft, if they catch you. They hardly ever do.

Redgenold

56th of Summer, year 111

It is clear that I cannot go on like this- aimlessly wandering, scouring the fields of dead for useful items. I'll starve soon anyway, as game is so scarce. I am still Haputian though, and what I am about to do seems nothing short of treason. It is this or my death, but Quip would never forgive me- even if she liked me to begin with. Another skirmish has left a dozen dead in an abandoned field. Four of them are Laitmean. There is one, about my size, who was killed by a kick to the head from a horse.

I tried not to look at his squashed face as I stripped his body. I now have an unbroken, mostly clean Laitmean uniform, sturdy boots, and a full kit. I am sorry, my dearest Quip, but I am Laitmean now. It is my only hope of living to see you again.

* * *

57th of Summer, year 111

I only had to walk a few hours before I came upon a company, different from the one decimated on the hill behind me, and seeing them about to set off, I called out. Their leader, a Second Lieutenant with a fantastically large mustache, rounded on me demanding to know my story. I explained that most of my unit had been killed by a group of Haputians before we could fend them off, and I had been knocked out in the chaos. Given the gash on my face, the story was at once accepted, and I was welcomed with open arms into their ranks, which were a few men short. That I have no military training matters little. Many of the soldiers in this area are just farm hands who signed up for some extra coin. I have now learned that this unit is being sent to Firdell to join a larger battalion. The invasion of the Capitol, I must call it Haputa's capitol, now I am Laitmean, is under way, and we are going to take Quirton and the surrounding towns once and for all- for the sixth time in recent months.

* * *

58th of Summer, year 111

I pick up the military ways quickly; they think I have been in the army for a while. Nobody questions me. I am now sure that it is the 58th.

* * *

59th of Summer, year 111

We are one day from Firdell, and an unspeakable thing has happened. Some knights from a nearby estate mutinied and charged us. The lead man screamed how Haputa would destroy us as he ran- he had been stripped of his sword and held a pitchfork. There were only three of them, and they were dispatched quickly, leaving two of our own dead, and three others wounded. A man called Crawly bandaged up his own arm and was going to help bury the two dead men, whose names I didn't know. Then he gave a cry and ran to the Second Lieutenant. We hadn't noticed it earlier in the chaos, but a tine of the pitchfork had punctured him deeply in the gut. The fork had manure on it so it was a matter of days before the gash turned sour, but he was spared the agony. We couldn't stop the bleeding, so he died a quicker death. This left the men in a disarray. They couldn't tie their boot laces without their leader telling them to, much less march to Firdell, even if it is only a day away. So I shouted at them to form up, and they did. Then Crawly said I should take the

139

Second Lieutenant's place. I feigned distress when Crawly took the uniform off the lieutenant, as if I hadn't done the same myself just a few days ago. So now I am 'leutent, Sir!' If only Quip could see me now.

The Warrior

Year 111, 61st day of summer

We reached the Capitol, and left Ettalara with Dart for the day, so that we could get supplies, by which I mean extra weaponry, 'cause the city is preparing for a siege. I reckon we should find the Senate soon, and tell them about the book, Ettalara, and *cough* Dart. TOP SECRET.

The Lady

61st of summer

We have entered the capital and are hiding out in an old building. So far I have not been allowed to leave which is maddening to say the least. I'm beginning to think it was a mistake to come here. I feel more like a prisoner than a spy.

The Thief

61st day of summer

Sorry, I had to distract Dart and never got back to my diary. Now, where was I? Oh, yes.

We eventually gave Lara her book back but we had to head into the city because Laitmean soldiers were coming. Lara was dragged with us in our hurry. Once we were safe inside the gates, Quip and I started looking for the Haputian Senate.

I listened at doors and eventually, in an old shack, we found them. They were sitting in the cellar. Quip kicked down the door and we sauntered in. Eyes went wide and jaws fell open. We must have been quite a sight.

Once the council got over their shock and our story was explained, Quip told them about Lara. I knew this was part of the plan, but couldn't help feeling slightly guilty. She had been through a lot with us. But, I pushed my feelings aside. *Act now, think later.*

"We have also trained a dragon for the armies of Haputa," Quip went on. "Since cannons aren't safe for a man to use, a dragon is ten times stronger and will survive even if the cannon blows up." Again, I couldn't help feeling slightly nervous about Dart manning a cannon. (It seems he was so small when we took him that he thinks I'm his mother, and I must say that sometimes I feel that way too.) Soon it was decided. Quip would take a few councilors and some guards to get Ettalara and I would take three councilors to Dart. If I tell him they mean no harm, he'll be perfectly happy to do as they say. We would meet at the gate.

When we reached the abandoned house where we had been staying, I heard a whimpering noise. Entering quickly, I looked for Dart. He found me first. Leaping to his feet, he darted toward me and I reached up to pat his nose. He greeted me like an eager puppy, all frolicky and wagging his tail. I was rather flattered but tried not to show it.

We left and headed toward the main gate, Dart beside me. Quip was there, her dagger at Lara's throat. Lara wriggled out of Quip's grip with a final despairing effort, but found her way blocked by guards and senators. She had a mix of emotions covering her face, anger, fear, and hurt pride. Although I still felt guilty about what we had done, I made sure to place a mask over my emotions like I had done most of my life.

Quip looked smug as we all marched down to the councilors hiding place. We're all sitting here waiting for the councilors to finish discussing things among themselves. It's hard to write quickly, but this task is made even harder because Lara's glaring so hard it looks like she could shoot fire out of her eyes.

"Now do you wish you'd run, while you could?" Quip asked Lara. Lara responded by turning her back to us. Quip leaned into me with an amused look and whispered, "she's ignoring us."

"Obviously," I said, rolling my eyes dramatically. Honestly, I'm still feeling a little guilty for what we've done, and I'm especially nervous about what questions the Senate will ask us. More later, they're done talking.

* * *

Later

Well, questioning has ended for all of us. Lara was taken into a separate room from Quip and I. There is nothing for us to do except to sit and wait while the council decides what to do with us. They are still talking. I wonder where Dart is. The faces of the men when I brought him out were priceless.

THE
SENATE

10

18 Your secret is safe with me
There was a secret so well kept
That those who did not know it wept.
Although it was well guarded,
The keeper was bombarded
'Til out the tale was cleanly swept.
There once was a secret well hid
And well-kept by lips with a lid
'Til as has been said before,
The truth got out of the door,
And all blame was placed on the kid.

The Lady

62nd day of summer

I've been betrayed. I never trusted Quip and Trill to begin with, but I never thought they would do this to me! I am so hurt and angry! After we got to the old building and spent the night, the girls went out to rob the armory for weapons. I went with them. Not because I wanted to steal, but because anything was better than staying in a room with that beastly dragon. Once they had broken in, Quip grabbed an ax, while Trill took a bow and several arrows.

Quip sent me back to the building to give the ax to the dragon to guard. I knew it was only an excuse to get me away, but I couldn't do anything about that. They told me to meet them by the wall once I was done.

I placed the ax where Quip had instructed, but the nasty dragon tried to keep me from leaving! I was beginning to wonder what else Quip and Trill had instructed him to do. He tried to block the door, but I dodged him, and made my way to the wall to wait for the others.

I had been there for maybe fifteen minutes when Quip came casually strolling by. She looked innocent. Quip looking innocent is a bad sign, as I found out.

"Where's Trill?" I demanded.

"Oh, that doesn't matter," Quip replied, "Lovely weather we're having, isn't it?" I began to edge away, but suddenly Quip slid close, put her arm around

147

me and pulled a knife close to my throat.

"Don't move," she ordered. Then I noticed Trill standing with the dragon just a few feet away and several men closing in. It was then that I fully realized what was happening. I was going to be captured! Quip and Trill must have told! I panicked, and grasping Quip's wrist, I jerked the knife away from me, slid out of her grip and backed away quickly, only to find myself surrounded by the soldiers.

We were all hustled off to a guard tower above the wall. There, we were told to put our weapons on the floor. I set down my bag, but only after I had slipped my knife out. I wanted to take out the book, too, but it was too risky to attempt without being noticed. My only hope was that they would not bother to look in the bag if I acted as if it didn't matter to me. I was surprised that Quip and Trill were being treated in the same manner as I, but I soon gathered from the conversation that the men who captured me were personal guards of members of the Haputian Senate, and they didn't quite trust the other girls yet. Apparently, they barged in on a very secret, very important meeting of the Senate, claiming to have information that would aid Haputa. Quip and Trill never were much for tact.

We were all questioned thoroughly. They asked each of us where we were from. Quip and Trill truthfully told their stories (at least as far as I could tell), and then it was my turn.

"Where are you from, and who are your parents?" An elderly man inquired.

"Well," I replied cautiously, "I imagine Quip and Trill already told you I'm from Laitmea, which is true." I decided to ignore the last question. But the man was persistent.

"Who are your parents?" he asked, more forcefully this time.

"Oh, nobody of importance," I answered, vaguely.

"What are their names?" he asked again, taking a step forward.

"Um..."I was saved from answering as one of the younger men, who had been going through my bag interrupted.

"Nothing but a comb, sewing supplies, and spyglass, but this is what really interests me," he said, holding up my book. I closed my eyes. Please, not the book.

"Ah," the older man took it and sat down. After inspecting it for a few moments, he spoke.

"These are very rare- king Darin of Laitmea had these given to all his noblemen in case anything happened to him. They contain information on the whereabouts of Laitmea's stash of weapons and treasure." I felt the blood drain from my face as murmurs rippled through the room. All the king's noblemen? Did this mean my book wasn't the only copy? I could have destroyed that book any time I wanted? I had insisted on carrying a leatherbound death sentence for nothing? Why had no one told me?

"The king now thinks it has become too dangerous to have these records, and wants to collect them and destroy them, lest they fall into the wrong hands," he continued, "The last known copy of this book was in the possession of the king's most trusted advisor." He turned to speak to me. "The inscription is addressed to you and signed by your mother. You are far from ordinary." He looked me squarely in the eyes. "Are you, or are you not the daughter of the king's Chamberlain."

I knew there was no point in lying, but even so, I hesitated before answering.

"I am," I replied, sullenly. Again, the whispering began. The man then turned and addressed Quip,

"Why did you not turn this girl in the moment you knew she was Laitmean?" He demanded.

"I didn't know exactly who she was," said Quip.

"Hmm," the man frowned, "We need to discuss this." He turned to the other members of the Senate and they began to talk quietly among themselves.

Quip and Trill also began to talk, but I ignored them. I feel terrible. Not only have I betrayed my country, I have also gotten myself and the book captured. In my fear for my own safety, I behaved rashly and threw away opportunity after opportunity to destroy it or at least get it away from Quip and Trill. I hate myself for my selfishness, and I am still frightened and angry. I doubt the Senate needs any more information from me, but even if they do, I know I couldn't withstand torture! I'll sing like a bird the moment they even wave a whip in front of me. Why didn't I get rid of the book the moment I had a chance? Why didn't I flee from Quip and Trill? Why did I trust them

149

at all? They used it against me. They betrayed me. I am absolutely livid, but also a bit sad. How could they, after all we have been through together? Do they care so much for Haputa that they will sacrifice any person, a friend (as I had almost grown to believe), for the "greater good" of their cause?

Finally, the Senate finished their discussion and came back to us. Quip and Trill were permitted to take up their weapons and fight. The Laitmean army was nearly upon us. I was told I would remain in the tower under guard until after the battle when they would decide what to do with me. So that is where I am now. They gave me back everything except, of course, my book.

They haven't tied me up or anything. I suppose they think there is no escape for me, which is probably true. Five guards are inside the room with me, and of course there are many more just outside on the wall. There are only a few arrow slits in the wall, obviously too small for me to fit through. This is so frustrating! I wish there was *some* way for me to escape! I could throw this journal down with a note inside, I suppose, but it would attract the attention of my guards. And I really don't want the entire army to read this whole thing. I can't stand at the window and call; the guards would just move me to another location. All I have is my spyglass, handkerchief, needle, some green thread...

Wait a minute. I have an idea!

The Damsel

What better deed could a knight do
Than vanquish a dragon or two?
Thought Sir Brone, not any, and so he set out,
To prove himself strong and stout,
(As knights are expected to be.)
People thought him lacking, you see.
He traveled far and wide,
But not a dragon could he find.
In desperation, he cried out,
"There must be *some* dragons about!"
And to his surprise, he got a reply,
A damsel, no word of a lie,
Who said, "Please hush,
Or the dragons *will* come, and turn you to mush."
He turned and saw her at the mouth of a cave,
Strikingly beautiful, strong and brave.
"There's a dragon, in fact, keeping me here,
But I'm quite afraid you can't rescue me, dear.
You see, this dragon, while now sleeping,
would die before I leave his keeping."
"No matter, I'll slay it", said Sir. Brone,

And drawing his sword he entered the dragon's home.
There it was, fast asleep,
And with one flying leap,
He struck with his sword most strong.
But the beast didn't die, it didn't even yawn.
It simply rolled over, pinning the knight,
Who, true to form, gave up the fight.
But the damsel said, "Ah, wait, I was wrong.
You *can* help me knight, for you aren't strong.
In fact you're so pitiful the dragon won't see,
If I give you my dress, he'll think that you're me!"
So she took his armor, his sword and his horse,
And left him in the cave, in her dress, of course.
And as far as I know, Sir Brone is still stuck,
Serving the dragon, with his rotten luck.

The Warrior

Year 111, 62nd day of summer

I suppose I can write about the Senate's secret plans now, since they won't be a secret much longer. So here's the deal. The Haputian senate, which has been on the run since the Laitmeans have been invading, came up with some top secret plans that they told to a bunch of Loyalists, and Trill and I found out about by listening at doors, which is fine, since we're loyalists too. They found a man who had designed a cannon that he thought would really work, but he didn't want to try it, 'cause cannons tend to blow up and kill the people firing them. So the Senate was going to try and tame a dragon to light the cannons for them, 'caus dragons don't mind explosions. Only everyone was too chicken to try and tame a dragon. So Trill and I decided to get ourselves a dragon, but we got captured first, and had to take the long way to Mer. Now we have a dragon, and now he's big enough to light the cannons (they made several, in the hopes of coming up with a way to light them from afar.) so we'll set up for a siege, and when the Laitmeans come, POW! Once they get by the gates Dart will come with the cannons and give 'em what they deserve. We talked it all over with the Senate, and they were rather skeptical, but they did get some answers out of Lara and now she's under lock and key, and Trill and I are with the archers. Trill feels a little bad about doing that to Lara I think, but I'm not so sure. I know she's a person an all, but really, did she do anything for us without thinking how it might benefit her? Maybe I won't go so far as to strangle her with my bare hands, but I'm pretty sure she'd sell us to the enemy at a moment's notice. We are also going to drop flaming pine logs on the Laitmeans heads.(My idea)

* * *

Later

Yes, I stabbed the handkerchief. Long story, fun siege, gotta go. Rocks to drop, DEATH TO LAITMEA!!!!!

Redgenold

64th of Summer, year 111

It is a good thing that Laitmea's army is so large, else the company at Firdell would surely notice that the Lieutenant coming in is not the same man that left. I have been put in charge of a larger fraction of men, as a First Lieutenant, no less. I have also been told to use any force necessary to get them to march. We are to take a village a little way from Quirton- I have been given a whip to use, as men tend to balk at removing people from their homes. My commander said to use it as much as I want. I recognize the man. A few seasons ago he was jamming me into a wagon alongside all the other poor orphans taken for slaves when Quirton was taken the first time. I cannot pretend that I was good to the little ones, but a man that would flog children- all I did was scare them to annoy Quip. He abused them and treated them as property. Both of us wronged the little orphans. I suspect an accident may befall him during the raid: penance for me, deserved punishment for him.

The Lady

65th day of summer

I can't believe it worked! I am free! Free! Here is how it happened.

Laitmean soldiers had begun to pour into the city, causing quite a lovely distraction. I put away my journal and took out my needle, thread and handkerchief. Then I began to stitch. At first the guards watched me curiously, but they soon grew bored with this and, thinking I was only stitching to pass the time, left me alone. I worked about a half an hour until I was finished. The handkerchief now held my cryptic message, with the location of the tower I was in, and a short note for help. I then stood slowly and casually made my way toward the arrow slit with the handkerchief in my hand. While I waited for there to be a break in the action, I wound the fabric into a ball, in an attempt to make it travel farther. Then, I saw my chance.

Peeking over my shoulder to ensure the guards were not looking in my direction, I threw the handkerchief as hard as I could. It came unraveled as it flew through the air, and did not make it as far as I would have liked, but it was far enough. One of the Laitmean soldiers spotted it and picked it up. He scanned it quickly, then looked up at my tower. I would have waved, but by now my captors were looking in my direction with suspicion, so I decided to move away from the window. I sat back down and began to put my belongings in order as innocently as possible.

Only fifteen minutes or so later, there was a great commotion outside and then the door was kicked in with a crash! Soldiers flooded the room and killed three of the five guards right away. The other two stood in front of me, fighting with all their might.

Then, two figures appeared in the doorway. Quip and Trill! Quip jumped in and killed a Laitmean soldier right away, and Trill began to fight, then was forced to turn and fight the other Laitmean soldiers trying to force their way into the room.

Another Haputian soldier fell so that only one was left to guard me. But suddenly, Quip was there too, and just in time as the last guard fell only seconds later. I was backed into a corner, Quip standing in front with her back to me. Quip fought fiercely; anyone who confronted her was stabbed or kicked back.

I realized that Quip could probably defeat all the Laitmean soldiers in the room single handed. Then what would become of me? And my country? Laitmea still had no idea that the Haputians knew the location of the treasury. It would be raided, and it would be all my fault! I wished that the Soldiers would hurry up and get me out of there.

Suddenly, I decided I was sick and tired of always being the helpless damsel in distress. I figured that unless I took action, I would never get out of there. I was still angry with Quip for turning me in. And so, without a second thought, I jumped on Quip's back, pulling her down. We fell to the ground heavily and I stayed on top of her until the Laitmean soldiers wrenched the knife out of her hand and pinned her down. Then I jumped up, smoothing my dress, and collected my belongings as the soldiers bound Quip and dragged her to her feet. I must say, they did not have an easy time of it. Quip was quite uncooperative and several of the soldiers had black eyes and bloody noses before they got her under control.

Then, we fled. On our way out, I saw Trill several yards away with the dragon. Her eyes widened when she saw Quip being dragged away and she started toward us, only to have her way blocked by more Laitmean soldiers who had broken through. We made it out without further incident.

Quip was taken to the prison tent as soon as we reached the Laitmean camp, but I was led to the Commander's tent. I gave him all the information I could think of, about the book, the Senate, and Quip.

"We'll be questioning her soon, but it doesn't seem she will be very compliant. Do you know what, if anything could make her talk?" the Commander asked.

I hesitated. I knew what might make Quip give the commander information. It would be awfully cruel… But then, she had betrayed me without a second thought!

"She has a friend," I began slowly, "A girl named Trilliapa, Trill for short. They are very close."

"Ah," the Commander's eyes glittered nastily, and I shivered. "What does this girl look like?"

"She's about my height, with dark curly blonde hair and blue eyes."

"Anything else I need to know?"

I thought for a moment before adding, "Yes. She has a dragon."

ARCHON

The Thief

66th day of summer

Oh, boy. I must write quickly because I need to prepare a rescue. The Senate agreed to let Quip and I help in the battle. I'm not sure if it's because they trust us or because they needed me to manage Dart. Anyway, we were positioned atop the wall. They weren't ready to fire the cannons yet, so I fought on the wall with Quip, who was happily pushing heavy rocks and logs down on the enemy. We were so busy, we almost didn't notice the small white object that flew out of one of the tower windows. I motioned to Quip and we both looked over the wall. A Laitmean soldier stopped and picked it up. He then looked up sharply and scanned the wall. Quip and I exchanged uneasy glances. The object was clearly a handkerchief. Who would throw something so dainty to the enemy? That's obvious. Ettalara.

The soldiers looked even more desperate to get into the city as the handkerchief was passed around. Quip and I flew down to the main gates right as they were forced open with a battering ram. We fought our way towards the largest group of soldiers, who were clearly meant to be Lara's rescue team. Most of them didn't look much older than fourteen and I think I even recognized a boy from the orphanage. What kind of army forces children to fight? Quip and I at least came here of our own free will. We ruthlessly fought our way through the crowd until suddenly, the offending handkerchief came into view. It was so filthy by now it was almost unrecognizable. Quip angrily stabbed it with her knife and lifted it up so we could see the message stitched upon it. Lara's initials were embroidered in green thread, along with the words, "the east tower." Quip muttered to herself words I was sure I didn't want to hear. We fought our way towards Lara's room. Laitmean soldiers were pouring in. Quip fought her way inside, but I was forced to remain on the wall to keep more soldiers from getting in. My truncheon knocked quite a few off their feet as I made my way towards Quip. Only I got there too late. By the time I entered the room, the Laitmeans were speedily dispersing, and Lara and Quip were gone.

* * *

69th day of summer

Whew! Sorry to leave you hanging, but I had to figure out a rescue plan, remember? To make a long story short, Quip was captured and taken to the Laitmean camp where she was tortured horribly. I have a new look on Lara. Sure, we betrayed her to the Senate, but she had no right to blab all about… everything! To her little band of snobs! We hadn't hurt her, and definitely would not have tortured her, yet she deliberately shoved Quip to them and allowed her to be abused! If I could turn her in again, I would, and without any hesitation or guilt this time!

After the battle, the Senators had a brief (by their standards, I swear I almost fell asleep near the end) talk about Lara's poem book, and it was decided that I should take Dart and a few loyal Haputians to raid Laitmea's treasury. This would cripple Laitmea, and give Haputa much needed gold. I did as I was told, and made an extra stop on the way back at the Laitmean camp to pick up Quip. The Haputian loyalists the Senate sent with couldn't do a thing about it, as we were all riding the same dragon, and he listens to me before anyone else. I must say, It was thrilling, soaring so high, and the men's screams were so comical, I forgot to be terrified that I was up in the air. Their faces when we retrieved Quip were even better! But enough of that! I don't have time to explain everything. More on flying later.

Anyway, in Quip's poor state (thanks to a certain someone), the plague returned. It was so bad, that even the thick-headed Laitmean Captain realized how deadly it was and ordered Quip and anyone in close contact with her to be executed. Lucky for her, I arrived just in the nick of time and we escaped from the camp as fast as Dart could fly. I didn't see Lara. She was probably feasting with all the other officers in celebration of Quip's death.

Quip is waking up and daylight is near.

* * *

Later

Oh, no! Remember how fragile Quip's condition was? Well she just became delirious and had to go to the hospital. I shall visit her as soon as I'm done training with Dart. I'm really quite fond of him and do hope nothing ever happens to him.

* * *

70th day of summer

Quip is so delirious she barely remembers our adventures together. She knew who I was but couldn't figure out how we got out of the orphanage. I brought blankets to her and extra food and even though she doesn't remember, I told her how training is going with Dart. He did very well lighting the cannons during the battle, but he still tries to eat gunpowder now and again. I'd better go now, Quip is calling for me.

* * *

Later

Ugh! Guess who I ran into? I was just putting Dart back in his stable, when low and behold, Miss traitor herself walked in. She looked like she was going into battle with a grim expression, determination etched on her face. When she saw me, a look of shock and horror overcame the determination though. I snatched up my truncheon and cornered her before she could react.

"What are you doing here?" I demanded.

Disdainfully, she threw her hair over her shoulders, rolled her eyes and crossed her arms over her chest. She wanted to look smug and imperious I think, but I knew she was just stalling for time to recover from her surprise. "None of your business," she snapped. Suddenly, she seemed to change her mind. "Actually, I came for my diary. Do you have it?" she demanded.

Inwardly, I snickered. Quip had stolen it before I rescued her from the Laitmean camp and I did my part by throwing it away. Into the ice cream cart. I loooove ice cream.

"I've looked all over! You must have it!" Lara continued.

I held up my hands innocently. "Don't."

She scowled at me in frustration.

"Dart!" I called. Lara had a panicked expression frozen on her face. She hates Dart. He obediently came to me. "Sit," I commanded, and he sat in front of Lara, blocking her into the corner. She started to protest, but I was already out the door. The Councilors would hear of this!

But when I returned with a couple of soldiers to show the spot, she was gone. "Blast!" I cried when we arrived. I was tempted to use the language Quip sometimes used when she was furious, but many young children had followed us to see what all the commotion was about, so I refrained.

I searched everywhere, but in vain. "Dart!" I ordered. "Come with me." Dart and I searched the hospital, market, and town square for two hours with the soldiers trailing uselessly behind. I was just about to give up, when a soldier started suddenly and pointed down a ways. "Look!"

I did. And there stood Lara, gazing down into the moat with a thoughtful expression. The water was rippling and I think she must have thrown something in. We overtook her before she knew we were there.

"Come with us," a soldier demanded and we escorted her away. When we reached the council, a man stepped out and informed us that the Senate couldn't see her right away and due to her recent escape, we should put her in jail for a few nights.

Better go. I hear commotion over by the hospital.

The Lady

74th day of summer

The Second Diary of Ettalara

Private Property of Ettalara Annalee of Firdell

If this does not belong to you, please do not read it. If your name happens to be Quip or Trill, I know you will keep reading this anyway, but just so you know, there is probably nothing in here you don't already know.

This is my second diary. The first one I had to throw into the moat because some certain painstakingly persistent people were after it. Thus, I shall endeavor not to make any more mistakes. This journal shall only be a record of all the strange events and people with whom I become involved. I shall disclose no information that is not already common knowledge within these pages to ensure this journal cannot be used against me.

I am sitting in a Haputian prison. There is little privacy and even less to do. Although since I have so much time on my hands, I suppose I should write about how I came to be locked in this uncomfortable place.

It's all thanks to Quip and Trill. When Quip was captured by the Laitmeans, she was tortured. (Contrary to popular belief, I did not know that was happening and would have intervened if I had. The commander insisted she was being treated decently and, like the fool I was, I believed him.) In her weakened condition, Quip fell ill with the plague. Again. Really, this plague business is most irritating. I think she meant to get sick, just to cause trouble! That would be just like her. After the Laitmean commander found out I had been in contact with her, I was locked up with Quip. She was there only for a little while, as they meant to kill her, but she still manged to steal my diary in that time. Then Trill came in and rescued Quip, just as she was about to be killed. They rode away on Dart just as suddenly as they had arrived.

The Laitmean Commander was still rather put out (to put it mildly) because I forgot to mention that Quip had been a plague victim. It simply slipped my mind with all the other important things that were going on! He was also upset because we had just gotten word that the Haputians, led by Trill and Dart, had indeed raided the treasury (apparently she rescued Quip on her way back from this escapade). So, I was stuck in the tent along with anyone else who had been in contact with Quip, and probably just so they could execute the first one to show symptoms. I was frantic to get out, so I did a very stupid thing. I cut a hole in the tent, crawled out, and snuck into the Haputian capitol in search of my diary.

It wasn't easy to sneak in, but once I avoided the main guards, I was able to get by pretending to be a weary Haputian peasant in need of sanctuary. They let me in immediately (very irresponsible, in my opinion), and for once I was glad I didn't look very intimidating. I was careful not to speak much, however, because I knew they would pick up on my accent.

After getting in, I first went into the barn where the horrid dragon was being kept, only Trill emerged at exactly the wrong moment, cornered me and then had the smelly dragon guard me while she went to tell the Senate (she had a truncheon so I could not object; I desperately need a foil). Fortunately, someone entered the stable without seeing me, and in the confusion, I slipped away.

I went to look for Quip. (This just goes to show how desperate I was.) I searched all the usual places before I realized she must be in the hospital. That is indeed where I found her, completely delirious. She didn't remember anything about me except that I was annoying, or so she claims. Honestly, the most annoying person I've ever met is Quip and nobody can top her! I could see she didn't know where my journal was, so I left.

I wandered the streets for some time before I saw the ice cream man emptying his trash. And there, in the middle of it, was my diary. I rescued it (it was smelly and soggy but all in one piece) and then I decided I probably shouldn't have it on me. I couldn't recall every detail that was in it, but I was fairly certain I would only be condemning myself if anyone read what was inside, particularly the Laitmeans. So, I pitched it into the moat where it promptly sank.

Just in time, too, as Trill and members of the Senate and some soldiers rounded the corner the next second. I was again captured, and I have been here ever since.

The only bright side to my situation is that I no longer have the book. At least it has ceased to put me in danger. I hope I never see it again.

They just brought Quip in and put her in the cell next to me. She must still be delirious because she put up quite a fuss (Then again, that could be a sign she is in her right mind). I heard some of the guards saying they caught her trying to burn down the hospital. Go figure.

The Thief

73rd day of summer

Oh my gosh! I ran to the hospital and found Quip rubbing two stones together trying to light the hospital on fire! She was so delusional she didn't recognize me. A soldier ran over to her and hauled her to her feet. She didn't even to fight back much, which really makes me worried about her. I tried to explain who she was, but he hauled her over to the jail anyways. He shoved her in a jail cell and told the jailer everything. I added my explanations to the hubbub. Quip managed to fall asleep, but Lara, who was two cells down, only buried her head in her pillow.

Finally, I convinced the men that Quip was just sick and delusional and didn't know what she was doing and they agreed to leave her be until she gets well. She will still stay in her cell until they hear otherwise from the Council.

* * *

74th day of summer

Visited Quip in jail. She wasn't any better. Lara looks bored stiff.

The Warrior

Year 111, 75th day of summer

The Laitmeans got me. Turns out Ettalara embroidered HELP or some such thing on her hankie and threw it to the soldiers so they'd come get her. I tried to stop them, but got eh, a little tied up. Anyhow, Trill came after me, but boy did she take her time! Apparently the Senate wanted her to do important war stuff, but that's no excuse. At least Laitmea's floundering for gold now. Laitmeans are cruel! I would have been fine, but the plague came back with a vengeance after they whipped me. I thought I was recovered, but apparently not enough, because I became delirious. Actually, I woke up in prison after I broke out of the hospital and went on a mad rampage. I don't remember much. Apparently I was found trying to light the hospital on fire. I must say, I'm rather proud of myself. Trill thinks it's all Lara's fault, but I really don't know if she has the guts for all that. My best guess is she just wanted out and back to her life of luxury, and anything that happened to me was just a happy surprise.

Unfortunately there is still a war going on, and I am still in prison.

The Lady

〜⟨∘⟩〜

75th day of summer

I am so bored! At least Quip has Trill to visit her once a day.

I have an idea. I am going to practice my sentence diagramming. Why? Because I am bored out of my mind. But mostly to annoy Quip and Trill if they ever decide to read this.

QUIP IS BEING TOO LOUD!

"Quip" is a proper noun, "is being" is the linking verb phrase, "too" is an adverb and "loud" is a predicate adjective.

2. DART, THE HORRID DRAGON, IS SMELLY.

"Dart" is a proper noun, "the horrid dragon" is an appositive phrase with "dragon" as a noun, "horrid" as an adjective, and "the" as an article, "is" is the linking verb, and "smelly" is the predicate adjective.

3. TRILL IS DANGEROUS BECAUSE SHE HAS A TRUNCHEON.

"Trill" is the proper noun, "is" is the linking verb, "dangerous" is the predicate adjective, "because" is the adverb, "she" is a pronoun, "has" is an action verb, "a" is an article modifying "truncheon," which is a noun.

4. I AM CONVINCED THAT QUIP IS INSANE.

"I" is the subject, "am convinced" is the action verb phrase, "that" is an adverb, "Quip" is a proper noun, "is" is the linking verb, and "insane" is the predicate adjective.

Still bored out of my mind. All I want right now is a good meal and a hot bath because I am absolutely filthy! Here is a list of the food I miss:

Roast beef

Chocolate cake

Mashed potatoes

Tea

Raspberry jam

Lemon pudding

Oranges

Eggnog

Now I'm hungry! All we get to eat around here is stew and hard dry bread without butter. I have a feeling Trill sneaks food in for Quip. Why she hasn't broken her out of here yet I have no idea.

The Thief

76th day of summer

Quip woke up early and looked so refreshed, I gave her a few pastries I "borrowed."

The Lady

77th day of summer

How long are they going to keep me here? Don't they realize I'm of no use to them? If they're holding me for ransom, I wish them luck because I don't think Laitmea will pay it. Without my father's position and wealth, I'm worthless to them.

Worthless. Isn't that how Quip and Trill see me? As a tool to be used to bring Laitmea down and nothing more? And yet, as I've sat here and reflected upon the past few days, I can't say my actions have been very different. I readily betrayed Quip and Trill upon my rescue. Granted, I was angry and not thinking clearly, but is that really an excuse? I had a chance to redeem myself and instead I made everything worse. Quip could be dying in the cell next to me for all I know just because I believed the Laitmean Commander! Filthy deceiver. Are more Laitmeans like him than I realized? Could I possibly have been wrong this entire time?

16

56 How could you?
How could you look me in the eye,
And tell me,
Tell me you were fine?
How could you tell me such a lie?
When I looked,
I could see your inmost thoughts,
Like writing in a book.
How could you stand and watch me die,
Leave me be,
Could you not see?
You hurt me when you lied to me.

The Thief

78th day of summer

I don't know if I did the right thing or if I need to go to an insane asylum. I freed Quip. She had gotten over her sickness and had become very weak. I had heard of many raids by Laitmeans on poor farmers, citizens of Haputa. They were destroying their property and slaughtering men, women, children, and livestock. The ones they didn't murder were carried off as slaves. I couldn't take it anymore. So, I freed Quip and we are going to get out of here as fast as we can. However, we must leave Dart. He is city property now and owned by the Senate. They need him. I've ordered him to obey the Senators, but obviously his first loyalty is to me. So if I ever need him back, I can just call for him. I'm still heartbroken at the thought of not seeing him for who knows how many days though. If I didn't think that others needed my help more, I don't think I'd ever leave him.

I gave Quip her knife and we escaped before they closed the gates for the night. We "borrowed" a horse and made it to a neighboring village. It was growing dark and Quip wasn't in good enough shape to travel the whole night. Thieves roam the roads and although I could easily fend them off, Quip couldn't. So, here we are. I must go to sleep. We will wander around town a little tomorrow, get food, and then keep going.

The Lady

78th day of summer

I'm out of prison! And on the run, unfortunately, but that is nothing new. Trill broke Quip out shortly after my last entry. The moment they were gone, I picked the lock and escaped. I realized after I had escaped that it will probably look like Trill set both Quip and me free. I honestly didn't intend to get them in trouble this time, but I suppose they can take care of themselves. Now I'm on my way to the nearest city. Hopefully Quip and Trill will be the only ones in hot water for once!

The Warrior

Year 111, 80th day of summer

Trill broke me out, but it turns out that a short while later Lara got herself let out, and now the Senate thinks that Trill did it, so now we're outcasts. Wanted posters and all. (Which wasn't on the list but should have been.)

The Lady

7th day of fall

I made it to a city late last night and I've been keeping mostly out of sight. I slept in a haystack in a farmer's barn and this morning I swept out his horse stalls in return for some bread and milk. I've just been wandering around since then, and I think I'll move on first thing tomorrow. I don't want anyone to catch up with me.

I hear a bit of commotion on the other end of town. I'm going to see if I can't get a better look.

Redgenold

7th of Fall, year 111

   That insufferable Ettalara girl broke my whip. I was under the impression that she was Laitmean, but since falling in with Quip and Trill- I do not know if they have inspired her to new heights, or driven her quite insane.

The Thief

7th day of fall

Oh horror of horrors! We saw Lara! Somehow she escaped the prison. I am too depressed to write. I'll tell you about our battle later.

* * *

Later

I have to write eventually, don't I? I must say something before I burst!

So, Quip and I made it to a city a ways away from the capital. We sought food and found shelter to spend the night. While the night watch men made their patrols, we smuggled our borrowed horse into the stables. Early the next morning, I grabbed us a few snacks for along the way. We planned on staying there until Quip had fully recovered. We wandered the market place with some money we borrowed. We got new shoes and I got myself a new belt to keep my dress from bulging. We were just about to grab some ice cream when a cry ran through town. Laitmean soldiers were in the city! Quip and I held our weapons and ducked into a nearby building to wait for the first group to come. When we didn't see them immediately, I climbed a lamppost to see where they were. It took me only seconds to see an entire army flood into the street just beyond ours. I stared closer and nearly fell off the lamppost. It couldn't Be! Redge in all his glory was leading part of a squad of Laitmean soldiers!

I slid down and shouted all this to Quip. She stared out at the oncoming soldiers gloomily. "Come on then!" She yelled and rushed at the soldiers coming our way.

Just when I thought things couldn't get any worse, we saw Lara. She was shoving her way through the crowd with ruthless determination, a terrified expression on her face. She saw us too and froze. We continued to fight on, but I kept an eye on her. She looked like she was going to come over to us, but then she seemed to change her mind. Whirling around, she began to run in the other direction. She didn't get too far, though, before a soldier rammed into her. She fell and a man and woman from the crowd rushed in front of her. I don't know if they were trying to help her or if it was an accident, but the soldier struck them down with his sword anyway. He moved on.

Lara sat on the ground still motionless. She was looking at the bodies in front of her with absolute shock and horror. Was she really this oblivious to what a raid looks like?

Lara seemed to suddenly come to and ran off before we could follow. We lost sight of her in all the chaos. When it was clear the city was lost, Quip and I retreated to higher ground. Lara had clearly come this way and she wasn't hard to track. We finally caught up with her and she was very angry that we followed her, but I could tell she was a little relieved, too. We made camp in the woods. We didn't ask how she escaped and she didn't tell us. Maybe it's better if we never know.

The Warrior

Year 111, 8th day of fall

When we tried to leave Haputa, Laitmea decided to ransack one of the border towns, and we had to fight our way out. And of course old Ettalara face showed up, and now she's coming with us to Styllyg. Oh, will I never get a break? On the plus side, we did get to kill a lot of Laitmeans. And they destroyed an entire village, and a whole ton of crops. I think Lara's a bit mixed up about the whole matter, seemed a little shocked to see her people behaving like, well, Laitmeans. So she's not as cold blooded as the rest of them. Still a little snob of a princess though, not saying I have any respect for someone who don't even know what her own people are doing. Reckon she'll just accept the fact that they're all murderers and not be bothered so long as she don't have to see them killing anymore. Was pretty happy with me getting whipped and kicked about in the Laitmean army's camp. FILTH. ABSOLUTE LAITMEAN FILTH.

The Lady

8th day of fall

It was Laitmean soldiers! They raided the city, burning things and stealing and murdering people left and right. I was weaving my way through the destruction, trying to avoid capture (or death), when I came across Redge himself, beating both soldiers and townspeople alike with a long, cruel whip.

Without thinking, I marched over to him and snatched the whip from his sweaty hands.

"What do you think you are doing?!" I demanded. "That is no way to treat people!" And with that, I broke the whip over my knee and stalked away. (On a side note, I was surprised it broke so easily, but it seems my fear and outrage must have given me newfound strength.) Redge was shouting furiously and glancing over my shoulder, I saw several soldiers closing in on me. I broke into a run and headed out of the city to a small grove of trees and long grass outside of town. They soon gave up the chase and I was safe. I stood on the hill overlooking the ruined town. How could my own people be so cruel?

Then I noticed two figures emerge from the fray with several soldiers in pursuit. Quip and Trill. Couldn't I ever get rid of them? I must admit, I was a little nervous at meeting them. Would they be angry at me for any trouble I caused them? I hoped not.

Soon they rounded the bend and came upon me.

"Ettalara?" they shouted in disbelief. I rolled my eyes.

"What are you doing here?" I asked.

"We had to evacuate the city," Quip replied as if this should be the most obvious fact in the world.

"Well, why did you come here?"

"There's nowhere else to go." I sighed and stomped away. When I had walked a few steps I glanced back. They were following me. I was both annoyed and slightly relieved.

We stumbled across a little grove of mulberry trees and the girls promptly began eating. I wandered over to where I could see the dilapidated town. The citizens were being driven out by soldiers like cattle. Soon the sky would be dark with the smoke of the burning city. How could my people do such a thing?

I began to hurry away, without waiting for the girls. I wanted to be alone to think everything over, yet it soon became clear that Quip and Trill were again following me.

"Why are you following me?" I asked.

"No where else to go," Quip replied. We walked on in silence for a few minutes before the path split.

"All right, you go that way and I'll go this way," I told them, pointing to the path on the right. I didn't particularly fancy the idea of wandering around on my own, but neither did I trust Quip and Trill after the incident with the Senate.

"Nah, it's too barren. We'll continue on this way," said Quip, smiling slyly at Trill. I sighed, and we kept on walking. Eventually, the path split again, so I made the same offer.

"Too many trees," said Trill with a grin. Clearly, they were intent on following me, so I kept walking resolutely. It occurred to me that they could be following me with the intent of turning me in to the Haputian authorities in order to regain their favor. I hoped to lose them somewhere, but this was not to be.

We reached a little building and decided to spend the night. I have developed a distinct dislike of abandoned buildings, but it was better than nothing. At least Dart wasn't in this one.

Quip and Trill sat on rickety little stools they found in the corner, but I slid warily to the ground, right next to the door. This way nobody could leave without my knowing about it.

As they were getting settled, Trill accidentally dropped her truncheon and I scooped it up quickly. Quip whipped out her knife, but Trill merely shrugged.

"She can't really do anything with it. There's two of us and I've got a knife," said Quip. Trill did not seem convinced.

I inspected the weapon carefully and then said,

"I guess it's about time to turn in."

Trill held out her hand.

"First give me my truncheon," she demanded.

"Why should I?" I asked. "How do I know I can trust you?"

"You don't," she snapped, "Now give it back." Trill reached for it again, but I jumped up and bolted to the door. I had just gotten outside when Trill caught up with me and grabbed hold of my arm.

"Let me go!" I demanded, twisting my arm this way and that, trying to free myself.

"First, give me the truncheon," said Trill, coolly.

"Not until you let me go," I said, still trying in vain to wrench my arm out of her ever tightening grasp. Seeing I was getting nowhere, and suspecting Quip would soon be there to help, I let my body go limp and fell to the ground, forcing Trill to let go. I sprang up and took off running, Trill in hot pursuit.

I ran for all I was worth. I could feel Trill right behind me, gaining, gaining! And then we came to a hedge, blocking any escape. Desperately, I hurled the truncheon over the top as hard as I could. It landed with a thud on the other side.

Trill began clawing her way through the hedge to get at it, and I ran back the way we had come. Scaling the first tree I saw, I climbed as high as I possibly could, hiding myself in the leafy branches, and waited.

Quip and Trill wandered around for a bit, but never found me. I stayed in the tree all night watching them search for me. They didn't seem to want to kill me, but neither were they making any effort to leave the premises. In a way it was the best outcome I could have hoped for, but I couldn't very well stay in a tree until they decided to leave, so, in the morning, I carefully climbed down and made my way back to the shack.

I sat there for a few minutes before the girls returned. They seemed surprised to see me. I smiled.

"What took you so long?" I inquired demurely. Quip sighed.

"Well, we should probably get moving," I said, rising quickly and walking out the door. The others followed without a word.

LADY
ETTALARA
ANNALEE
OF
FIRDELL

Redgenold

9th of Fall, year 111

After ransacking the village- and that is no overstatement, it was nearly obliterated, we rejoined the main bulk of our forces at Quirton. This lot was far larger than anticipated, as it seemed the invasion of the capitol had gone badly. Horrendously, actually. Laitmea has only a few cannons, guns, and other such explosives, as they are expensive and volatile. Until recently, Haputa had fewer. But one cannot deny that their most recent design has been a complete success. Not only is it larger, and less likely to explode at inopportune moments, they had a dragon to light the fuse, so no one would get killed if things went south. Dare I guess how they got such a thing? But that is not what is important. When we reached Quirton, I sought out my Commander, that same dirty slave rat I've wished dead for weeks and weeks. That he recognized me in the end was undeniable. The look of utter horror in his eyes- I killed him cleanly, though I would have liked to draw it out- I am not so cruel as he. When some other men came upon the body I had a surprise. Not knowing all the ranks of the army, I did not realize that I, even I, was next in command, and thus at the Commander's death, I've been promoted. It must never come out that I killed him, or people shall think I did it on purpose.

* * *

13th of Fall, year 111

We march to Laitmea's Capitol, meaning *the* Capitol today. I should say, some men march. For those of us who must be there soon, including us commanders, there are wagons, then a boat to take us down the river. I must stop being amazed at the food, the silverware- I must act as if I've lived with money all my life. This whole charade is becoming much more complicated than I intended. All I wanted was Quip's love-

* * *

20th of Fall, year 111

I have come to realize that I cannot pine away over Quip. That I love her is undeniable, but my attempts to get her attention are what drives her away. From now on, I shall behave myself, and try to be the sort of lad she'd like back. If ever we meet again- if not, I can just as soon find some rich Laitmean noblewoman to woo. I'll improve on my dancing for a start, and perhaps my position. My success thus far has been due mostly to luck, but if I want further good to come my way, some acting is in order. I'll start by mastering the waltz.

The Warrior

Year 111, 22nd day of fall

   She doesn't even know how to swim! Lucky for Lara, Trill is nicer than me, and pulled her out of the water. As if I was supposed to know that Lake Styll was so choppy. We got blown right back to where we started. So anyhow, Lara is still with us, which is ok, because she seems to be having a change of heart. At least I think she's telling the truth. Apparently her penniless noblewomen bit was just for show, and she does have some money. Believe it or not, she'll actually share. Perhaps now that she's seen her people slaughter countless innocents, she's figured it out. Took her long enough. Still not her friend though, and still a little skeptical.

The Lady

23rd day of fall

We walked on for a way until we came to Lake Styll. There we found a small fishing boat. The girls wanted to use it to cross the lake, but I was reluctant. I can't swim, for one thing, and even if I could, my heavy skirts would pull me right under. Eventually, Quip and Trill convinced me to get on and we began to cross.

At first, the water was calm, the wind blew gently, and the sky was blue. I began to relax. But the pleasant atmosphere disappeared when we were about half way across. The sky grew dark and stormy. Rain poured down, lightning flashed, and thunder boomed. The waves became choppy.

All of a sudden, a huge wave swept over the deck, and we were all thrown into the water! I, of course, cannot swim, and with the added weight of my skirts, I found I was sinking quickly. The more I kicked and struggled, the more my dress twisted about me, making it harder to move and stay afloat. I hadn't gotten a very deep breath before I went under, and my lungs were already burning.

Just as I had given myself up for lost, I felt someone tugging me to the surface. A moment later, my head came up above the waves and I drew in a long breath and started to cough. Trill (for it was she who had rescued me) pulled me back to the boat and I managed to get myself over the railing and onto the deck. Trill landed with a thud next to me and a moment later, Quip joined us.

As soon as I had recovered, I turned to Trill and said,

"I suppose I should thank you for saving my life."

"No problem," she returned.

What strange girls these are! One minute their only goal is to get me captured, and the next, they're saving my life! I fear I shall never understand them. It did make me feel better about things, though. If they are willing to rescue me from a watery death, then perhaps they don't intend to turn me in again (not that I would let that happen this time).

We managed to get the boat to shore without incident, but rather than try to cross the lake again, we sat down and talked, trying to figure out what to do. Clearly we needed some kind of direction or purpose. I for one was no longer interested in mindlessly wandering through the Haputian countryside.

"Well, what now?" Quip asked.

"We can't stay in Haputa, that's for sure," said Trill.

I thought for a moment. Perhaps the time had come to reveal the truth about my wealth. There was always the chance that things would go wrong and I would lose everything, but if I played my cards right, I felt I had a fair chance of coming out all right, and maybe even making things better for my country. That's what made up my mind. I had done enough blundering that only made things worse. Now I finally had the chance to fix things and do what was right!

"We could go to Laitmea," I said slowly.

"Why?" said Quip.

"I may or may not have extra money hidden there," I replied.

Quip sighed dramatically. "And I was just beginning to trust you!" I only smiled.

"So, what's your plan?" Trill asked.

"Well, with all the money I have, we could certainly purchase a small mansion near the capital along with a cook, a maid or two, a carriage, several horses, and plenty of good food and elegant gowns. That would enable us to get right into high society, something few Haputians have the ability to do. When the time is right, we strike. The nobles will never know what hit them."

"Where in Eretz did you get all this extra money?" Trill inquired.

"It was my mother's. It's not a commonly known fact that she was actually princess of Laitmea before the king stripped her of that title."

Quip and Trill stood agog. "Wait a second," Quip began, "you mean to tell us that we've been traveling around Eretz with the princess of Laitmea?! And we didn't turn you in? You should have told us!"

"It's not the sort of thing one goes around talking about," I retorted, "and anyway I'm not really a princess. Like I said, my mother was stripped of that title due to some family disagreement, I don't know the details. At any rate, she told me to only use the money in the case of an emergency, but I didn't use it when they died because delivering the book to king Darin was more pressing. However, I think my mother would agree that now is indeed the right time to use it."

"It sounds like you've changed sides," Quip remarked as we rose to begin our journey. I pursed my lips and considered.

"I'm not against my country," I decided slowly, "just the people running it. If I can help bring about their downfall and place good leaders in command, leaders who will respect other country's boundaries and look to become allies rather than take them over, then that will make everything we've been through worth it."

The Warrior

Year 111, 23rd day of fall

Lara grows ever more mysterious. As best I can tell she isn't so happy with the way Laitmea is being run, but doesn't have the guts to do anything about it, so she's sort of half asking us to fix things for her. Namely, she'll give us money and get us into Laitmean high society. So we can spy on all the nobles, and maybe poison a few. Certainly to pass information to Haputa, and win this war, and so on and so forth. Either that or Lara will betray us. She'll probably blackmail us to get in a position of power anyway. I was worried that we might not be able to get in touch with Haputa any more, after all they think we let Lara out, but then Trill pointed out that Dart is a dragon. Besides being obvious, that fact is why I agreed to the plan. Because Dart has imprinted on Trill, he'll be able to find her anywhere if she calls for him. The Haputian Senators will just have to deal with it when he vanishes and comes back with top secret information. I hope Lara knows I want Laitmea completely destroyed. One might wonder how she wouldn't know after traveling with me so much, but really, this is Lara we're talking about. I'm not sure she knows which way is up.

Redgenold

23rd of Fall, year 111

In reviewing my last entry, I see that I implied that these decisions have come about of a sudden, when in reality, it is all these days of brooding aboard this accursed frilly tea pot of a boat that have wrought this change. It vexes me to be aboard, though I am not rowing. I still have chain scars from my last time at sea. I have been neglecting to write, despite ample time to do so, but it is not mere negligence, a plot has been forming in my mind. Rumors abound aboard the ship, not least those about the captain of the guard- but more on that later. This day my lament is the silverware, namely that there is so damn much of the stuff. Pardon me. Such musings have no bearing on my life- save that I must learn such things as how to use the forks of nobility without disgracing myself. Laitmeans put such high stock by these things that a slip in court will ruin my chances of ever rising higher than Commander. I am only thankful that I am not a lady. I have no idea how Laitmean girls manage to have such small waists, but given their stiff manners, I don't doubt it hurts. I need only master the doublet and hose, and I am fearfully glad that neck ruffs have gone out of style.

The Thief

24th day of fall

Wow! You'll never guess where I am!

We made our way along the River Styll and, after a disastrous attempt to cross the lake, found shelter to talk. We talked a *lot*. We found out Lara's desire is only to get her property back. She warmed up to us so much we found out she has a secret hoard of money on her property and all we need to do is help her get it. We would be disgustingly rich.

Quip and I formed a plan of our own. We have made an agreement with Lara that we will help her get her money if she turns us into Laitmean noblewomen so we can get close to the important Laitmean nobles! Then I can call Dart to me, and send Haputa all kinds of information, like where Laitmea will strike next, and who to kill to cripple the nation. Although it would be a perfect spying opportunity, it took more than that to convince me to get suffocated in a pink dress in a room full of snobs.

"Just think," Quip whispered, "Gallons of ice cream, all for you!"

I paused and considered silently.

"Fine," I said, with an eye roll nearly as good as Ettalara's.

Redgenold

24th of Fall, year 111

Now that I have arrived in the Capitol, I shall attempt to make some account of the talk I heard aboard the boat. Now that Quirton and all the West of Haputa is under control, the excess of our troops, and those too high ranking for peacekeeping duty, have been brought back to garrison in Lyrah, to await muster and another invasion of Haputa's capitol come spring. Among the commanders, rumor is rife regarding the Captain of the Guard's failure. To not capture Archon, when we had such superior numbers and arms is a great disgrace, even in light of the new cannons, but perhaps not unpardonable, if the king is in a gracious mood. It seems though, in addition to such a loss, there was some snafu involving a prisoner of war ill with plague. Laitmea has fought the disease as hard as Haputa's soldiers, and not without success. If the man is found responsible for one of the most recent outbreaks, his doom is coming. To not immediately dispose of a plague baring prisoner is a crime punishable by death. His fall does not ensure my rise, any more than that of any other commander, but if he is removed, we all may have the king's eye on us.

* * *

26th of Fall, year 111

The first test: A banquet at the palace to welcome the returning commanders. I am decked out in a vest, tunic, hose, and soft soled shoes. My palms
are slick with sweat.

* * *

29th of Fall, year 111

The banquet went well enough. I have been fully accepted into Laitmean
society, enough that I may relax a bit into my role. Though I am a Commander,
I am not one of the king's pets, so I have much work to do if I wish to advance
myself. Of course I could simply work to get into his good graces, but that is
a slow going process. The other means of gaining favor are quicker, if not
as safe. To blackmail or frame for a crime one of the existing favorites is a
surefire way, as long as you are not caught. If you are found out- there is
a death penalty on blackmailers. So then that is too dangerous. The only
option that seems good to me is to catch someone in actual wrongdoing. The
object of everyone's scrutiny is, at the moment, the Captain of the Guard.
After his miserable failure at Archon, even the smallest slip of etiquette would
bring him down. And this is where I have an advantage. While king Darin
does not have any grounds to excuse the Captain of the Guard from his
duties outright, he has moved the man to a less glamorous quarter of the
palace- the Commanders' Hall, the suites across from mine. The others have
suddenly become very fond of me, always inviting themselves over to try to
spy upon my neighbor. But they do not see much. I make sure to be too busy
to entertain when the Captain is about. I *am* busy- watching his door.

The Warrior

Year 111, 30th day of fall

Now we are headed to Laitmea, in a carriage, no less, and Lara is blathering on about dessert forks and long vowels and I suppose we have to know all this if this half-baked plan has even the slightest chance of working, but ugh. And now I can't do run on sentences either. Shoulda fed Lara to Dart when I had the chance, but then we wouldn't be getting into Laitmea, so, that's that, I guess. Have to put up with her.

Redgenold

31st of Fall, year 111

My sleepless nights peeping out the crack twixt door and floor seem to be rewarding me. My target has become overly fond of one of the servants; I plan to speak with her today.

* * *

32nd of Fall, year 111

In Haputa, flirting with a maid is far from an unforgivable offense. But here, the gap between servant and master is too great a space to safely traverse. Slave, Beggar, Peasant, Servant, Freeman, Medic, Lord and Lady, Duke, Count, Guardsman, king, Advisor, Jester. I fear the poor girl near collapsed when I drug her off to give an account of the man's behavior. She needn't have feared, they shan't punish her, but the Captain of the Guard is Captain no longer. One should never say sweet things to a maid where prying eyes and ears might find. He needn't even kiss her, and he's gone too far. But then, the king was looking for excuses. The man could have sneezed the wrong way and been sacked.

* * *

34th of Fall, year 111

I have become the king's pet overnight. He is still wary of trusting a newcomer, but now I have a chance. Strangely, crown prince Dowlin has become interested in the Captain of the Guard business. He says he merely wants to know how things are done, as he shall be king one day, but I wonder at his motives. At sixteen, he's all the talk of the girls, as is Donis, who is a year younger. This means that there are a good deal of formal balls held. The king has desperately been searching for suitable wives for both of them. Dowlin, rumor has it, will have none of it. Some say he's holding out for a princess, but I've seen him dance. He just wants somebody who can keep a conversation going. Every other Laitmean girl has a head full of air, and the ones that don't have heads of rocks- But enough of that. The question is, why should someone as smart as Dowlin be interested in who becomes Captain of the Guard? He already knows exactly how things work, so his alleged reasons are false. I can only assume that he wants to somehow influence the outcome of this dogfight. The other commanders are attacking each other like beasts, trying to win favor. I stay out of it. If I attack no one, on one will have cause for vengeance.

The Lady

39th day of fall

We traveled for several days before we came to my home. Someone else was living there, but they hadn't changed it much, at least from the outside. It was a beautiful day, sunny, with a light breeze that cooled us as we sat on a rock overlooking my old estate. Oh, how I miss it! Someday, when this is all over, I'm going to buy it back. I would pay any price they ask if only I could have my rightful home again.

We found the money and carried some with us, leaving a little of it in its hiding place to be used later.

Prince

A prince is a man with very fine taste,
Well mannered and civil and true of heart,
He is of good breeding and speaks not in haste,
He is handsome and has an eye for art.
He treats every man well and with respect,
He is a good dancer, light on his feet,
In bearing and deportment most perfect,
And with all women he is kind and sweet.
When trouble comes he meets it like a lion,
Unafraid of doing wrong to defend
His people. As unyielding as iron,
He is courageous till the very end.
All this he must be and very much more,
For he'll be king like his father before.

Redgenold

41st of Fall, year 111

So Dowlin, it seems, will back me. It's all a rather odd turn of events. There was a banquet today for the marriage of some nobleman's youngest daughter, such a grand affair that half the city turned out to see it. In a gesture of unparalleled kindness, the man even allowed some of the less well to do, merchants and tradesmen, mainly, to join the festivities. Commanders do not mix with such rabble, so I was seated beside Dowlin, with a nameless pretty girl at my other hand. For much of the day, the Prince ignored me, forcing me to speak with the girl. Then, halfway through the second soup course, he turned to me, and said in a quiet voice, "You are Haputian, aren't you. You hide it very well, but the accent comes through now and again." I was too stunned to respond, but before I had time to panic, he added, "A Haputian guardsman might be useful." Then returned to ignoring me. The rest of the day passed in a barely remembered blur, ending when I returned to my quarters to find a missive on my table. It says that I have been appointed Captain of the Guard, and must report to his majesty tomorrow morning. And now my head is spinning too much to write another word.

* * *

42nd of Fall, year 111

I may know that Dowlin is behind my sudden rise to power, but the others do not. The Commanders are terrified of me, for they do not know how I managed it.

* * *

45th of Fall, year 111

Any thought of finding a rich noblewoman has left me, I wish so that Quip was here. These balls are tiresome, but I have learned from them. Flirting and eyelash fluttering and kissing is not love. Many a noble is wed to a girl he thought he loved and now despises- relationships must be built on love, not passion, else they crumble. If ever I see Quip again, I shall love her truly, not flirt or preen like a peacock.

Donis

Dorulin

THE
PRINCES

The Thief

52nd day of fall

    We are in an enormous mansion. Lara took one look at it while Quip and I stood in awe and said, "What a piece of trash! No wonder someone was selling it! It's a dump!" She got straight to work. Truth be told, as annoying as she is, I don't know how we would ever get close to the king of Laitmea without her. She knows it, too. She's been hiring servants and buying all sorts of things that are "absolutely essential" to life as noblewomen. Quip and I will start training tomorrow.

The Lady

52nd day of fall

We have bought a small, eight-bedroom home with only two staircases and a small stable, situated on about thirty acres of land. While not as grand as the home I'm used to, it does seem a luxury after traveling so much. Quip and Trill (who's names we changed to common Laitmean names, Evayah and Addmaleta) had never seen anything like it and had a hard time restraining themselves from touching everything in sight and even pocketing some of the smaller trinkets "to be used later."

Each of us has retired to our bedchambers and I'm writing this while sitting on my bed. It is so nice to have a clean satin nightgown and soft feather beds with fresh sheets and real pillows! Oh, how I have missed all this!

207

The Thief

53rd day of fall

AAAAAAAAAAAAAAAAAAAAAAAAAAAA!!!! How does one wear a… what do you call it? Let me ask Quip… Ah, a corset! I CAN'T BREATHE!!! I knew we couldn't do this. Lara says it's the height of fashion, but I think it's just a ladylike way of committing suicide! Quip, I think, feels the same way, but she doesn't show it.

Redgenold

53rd of Fall, year 111

Things move slowly. I have demanded that Laitmea have cannons to match Haputa's by spring, so that we might take Archon as soon as the snow clears, but until then, there is naught to do. About the most exciting thing to occur in recent days is the arrival of three noblewomen in town. One is named Ettalara, but her companions are not Quip and Trill- not that they could be noblewomen anyway. If I am invited to one more dance, I shall scream.

The Warrior

Year 111, 53rd day of fall
    slip
    stockings
    garters
    petticoats
    pocket
whatever the heck I'm supposed to put on next.

How on earth does Her Annoyingness keep track of all this? I can't!!!! Laitmea better die quickly, or I will.

And why do they need so many forks???

I AM DONE BEING A SPY. DONE. I'M FINDING TRILL AND GETTING OUT.

Well, maybe not, but that's what I *FEEL* like doing.

DEATH,

DEATH,

DEATH,

TO LAITMEA!!!

The Lady

65th day of fall

We have been invited to our first ball! It is a small affair, probably only one hundred people or so, but it will be good practice for Quip- Evayah and Addmaleta. (I am going to refer to them with their Laitmean names so that I don't forget and call them Quip and Trill in public.) They don't even know how to dress themselves! I had to help them, rather than risk the maids becoming suspicious because of their ignorance. I've been telling them about table manners, and which utensils to use and when and what makes pleasant dinner conversation. Trill-Addmaleta doesn't seem to pay much attention, but Evayah, for once, is actually trying to learn how to behave. Perhaps I shall make a Lady out of her yet.

The Thief

66th day of fall

I haven't been able to write much because I've been learning how to walk, talk, act, ride, breathe, and converse like a Lady. I have homework too! I must study a book about which spoon, fork, and knife to use, and how dinner parties work. We have our first party in two days and Quip and I have been going mad over it. Well, maybe Lara, too. She is trying anything she can think of to help us and, with my obstinate ways, is quickly losing patience.

* * *

67th day of fall

The party is tomorrow and Lara is a nervous wreck. I'm still mixed up on the dance steps to the minuet, and neither Quip nor I can remember the order of the infamous layers of clothing. Lara gave us some more etiquette books to read while she went to bed early with a headache. Quip is diligently studying her book over on her bed (oh, wait, actually I think she's asleep), but I've given up and decided to write a little. I must say, I don't think I've been this nervous in my whole life. Not even when going into battle knowing I may never come back.

The Lady

68th day of fall

I was being overly optimistic when I wrote that last sentence. Evayah has no desire to become a lady and I doubt she ever will.

The dinner went well for a first attempt. There was only one slight mishap when, during dessert, Addmaleta took the spoon of the person next to her by mistake and when Evayah pointed it out to her, started to laugh so hard that she actually put her head under the table. Fortunately, Evayah was able to make it look like Addmaleta was just choking, and I don't think anyone noticed so the crisis was averted.

Oh, the only other thing that happened was during the dancing when Evayah and Addmaleta decided to dance together and then when we switched partners, I ended up with Evayah. I was very angry and told them so in no uncertain terms all the way home, but I don't think they were a bit sorry.

The Warrior

Year 111, 68th day of fall

So we have to go to all these formal dinners with Lara, and yes, it's a hassle, and I have to wear heels and whatnot, but we do gather intelligence, and learn about Laitmea's strategies, and all sorts of stuff that Haputa can use to win this mess of a war. Only Trill was having a little trouble wrapping her noggin around it, so I said to her, (in my best Haputian drawl, long r's and all, but real quiet like,) "if ye behave yerrself, Ih'll dance wit ye at t' party" 'caus Lara's been real clear that we're not to make fools of ourselves, or dance if a boy don't ask us. After that, she perked up nice, and kept it together 'til dessert, when she went and grabbed the wrong spoon. I set it right, and made it come off like she choked when she were laughing. Lara wasn't too pleased, but no one noticed. So I offered Trill my hand for a dance, and when the partners switched, I ended up with Lara, and she looked about to kill me, but didn't, 'cause there was lots of young "gentlemen" looking on, and it wouldn't have been proper. She let us have it in the carriage home, but Trill and I tuned it out. It's not like I'd do anything too bad, I do want to bring Laitmea down.

The Thief

70th day of fall

First party was actually kind of fun. I wore pink and lace, but other than that, had a great time. We had a crazy amount of food to eat and I had to try to remember table manners. Quip seemed to be remembering everything and was having no trouble at all.

I was trying so hard to be perfect, I didn't even notice what I'd done until Quip pointed it out. She leaned over and whispered, "You grabbed the wrong spoon." I looked and realized I had taken the spoon from the man next to me. Fortunately I hadn't eaten much from it and Quip was able to slip it back to him discreetly. The man didn't notice and used the spoon without looking to see what we were smiling about. I started to giggle and couldn't stop. So, I stuck my head under the table, much to the amusement of Quip who made it seem like I was choking instead. When I recovered, I looked at Lara. Her eyes were closed, her hands were clenched, and she was mouthing something. Either a prayer of deliverance, or she also knew words not meant for a Lady such as herself. Quip and I had a good time with that. But when we came home, we got a good scolding.

The Truth

Sir Brone
Was well known
As the worst knight around,
Better off dead, or at least underground.
Yet it seems he's changed of late-
Got it in his helmeted pate
That he's supposed to be bold and brave and true,
Not idly sit, but go, and do!
His armor is polished, his horse fat and sleek,
He slays fearsome dragons, stands up for the meek.
In fact, some have said he's not the same man.
So some bards tried to pinpoint when it began.
Round new year, they say, he went out on a raid,
Let's go find the dragon he supposedly slayed.
For since then he has been such an exemplary fellow,
Whatever he found certainly made him less yellow.
So they went, bards and countrymen on a quest of sorts,
Through towns and cities, downs and ports,
Till they found the lair of a beast most grim,
And, when they looked therein-
Shock! Scandal! Sir Brone himself, serving the dragon.

He hadn't killed it at all, he was polishing flagons.
"Help Help!" He cried, when he saw the hoard,
"Save, me please, I'm bored!"
"No can do," Said lead bard, "I'd get in big trouble."
"But what's going on? I'm seeing double!"
"And why are you in a dress?"
Called another, "We thought you were rescuing damsels in distress!"
"I am, or I was, but we just traded places.
I got her clothes, she took greaves and bracers.
Then she ran away and left me to slay
This beasty, though how, I can't say."
"So the knight that we've seen," Said a bard, ignoring Brone's crying,
"Is a girl, not a man? That explains a lot." And he turned away sighing,
"We all prefer her, so if you don't mind,
Please stay here, it would be ever so kind.
Dame Brone covers all of our knightly needs, so you'll do more good
Taking care of our dragon, if you would.
I'm glad to see you've gotten your just desserts, good bye."
Said the dragon, "Get back to cleaning, else you die."

Redgenold

69th of Fall, year 111

Being sixteen makes me of a most desirable age, and newly minted bachelor. I have taken to fleeing at the sight of girls my own age, particularly her Ladyship Arabell of Lifeth, who has all the wits of a soup spoon and the charm of a rabid skunk. I pray the latest snowstorm shall freeze me in 'til spring. Prince Dowlin says much the same, as he has recently attracted the attention of a Lady Sylva, who is cousin of Arabell, but might as well be her twin. King Darin has almost lost his enthusiasm for match making, the girls here are so hopeless. Quip could teach them all a lesson or two. Speaking of the king, scandalous rumors abound. Some say he killed his queen, Elisabet. I wonder if it is true, but I daren't ask Dowlin, for she died when he was only seven, and it is most likely a painful memory. Having never known my mother, I cannot relate.

The Thief

74th day of fall

    We had so much fun at the dinner party, that we begged Lara to take us to another ball. Aside from the good food, you can "borrow" a lot of money and trinkets along the way. I even got a ring off my dancing partner last time.

    Lara said we haven't been invited to any more balls, so Quip told her to host one. She looked shocked like… how dare we suggest such a thing. We let it go - for now.

    So right now I'm sitting in a tree. There's a story about that, but I hear someone coming. Probably to find me and make me put on those ridiculous shoes. And hat. And gloves. Let's not forget the corset and parasol. (I snuck out in my slip.) Uh, oh, been spotted. Bye.

AAAAAAAAAAAAAAAAAAAAAAAAAAAAAAAAAAAA!!!! Horror of horrors! Death to the person who thought of etiquette! Death to anyone who defies me! DEATH TO FASHION!!!!!!!

Sorry, I've got control of myself again. I had to tighten my stays and pull up my stockings extra high and study etiquette books for young ladies as punishment for running off. Quip seems to enjoy my suffering. But she is having trouble with her corset which I enjoy tightening extra hard for her.

The Warrior

Year 111, 74th day of fall

   She ran off in stockings and a slip to avoid a pink dress. Trill, that is. It was the only thing with long sleeves clean for her, and in short sleeves anyone could see she's marked a pirate. That would spell disaster as sure as D-i-s-a-s-t-e-r does. So to get Trill to behave after today's ridiculous (and need I say dangerous) episode, I got her a nice new pair of shoes. Nice high heeled shoes. Five inch heels, to be correct. Got to spend the day gettn' ready for another party. Some important people will be there, so I'll keep my ears open. Maybe I'll get some information to send to Haputa.

Redgenold

78th of Fall, year 111

Alas and alack, the snow has cleared all too soon, and I must try to drown my sorrows in Laitmea's watery wine if I am to shake Arabell. Dowlin advises against playing a drunk, for even a drunk man can be rich. I do not yet know why the Prince takes such an interest in me, but I may take his advice-squandering wages on gambling is a sure way to lose a girl. There is no way to pretend to lose at cards though, and I am not that desperate yet.

The Thief

78th day of fall

Quip and I are ecstatic! The Royal family of Laitmea is hosting a masked ball in a week! Quip and I are determined to go, but Lara says we're not ready. I will work extra hard to get to that ball! If we don't, we will have lost a chance of completing our mission of p- Whoops! Not supposed to tell. I will train doubly hard if I can just make it in!

* * *

79th day of fall

Ha! We have been invited to the Royal Ball and when one is invited, one can't refuse! Lara is angry, but Quip and I just smile through her rants. We are training hard. Quip snuck into my room a few times to take a break. I don't think she's holding up very well. If it weren't for my sheer determination to get to that party, I would strangle the next servant to walk into my room.

Redgenold

79th of Fall, year 111

Masquerade ball my foot. I do not know why I should go- everyone knows me enough that a mask shan't hide me at all. The king is simply trying to get his sons to pick girls so he can get them off his hands. But then, I am tired of being abed and perhaps Arabell is slow enough not to recognize me in a mask -I could dance with some other girls and avoid her entirely.

The Lady

90th day of fall

We're attending a masquerade ball at the palace tonight! I've been to the palace several times, but never for a party. Evayah and Addmaleta are just excited about the masks. And about any information they can gather, but mostly about the masks.

Redgenold

90th of Fall, year 111

The palace has been aflutter all day to ready itself for the ball. Both princes are strutting about in new clothing- Dowlin in royal blue with cream colored trim, Donis in baby blue with garish gold roses- small wonder the girls flock to the elder brother. Save that Dowlin has dark brown hair, and Donis light, they are all but indistinguishable with glittering blue masks on. I am in my room, bracing myself for the ordeal ahead. My mask is black, as is the whole of my garb for the evening, save my shirt, which has slashes of red. I feared it might seem morbid, but the look is rather dashing if I do say so myself. Ah well, it is time.

The Warrior

Year 111, 90th day of fall

So this is a new one on me- a masked ball. We all dress up and go, but nobody knows who else is there. It's at the palace, so all sorts of royalty will be there. It seems like a good time to do a bit of snooping. Both of Laitmea's princes will be there, along with the king. Unfortunately, all the food is pre-tasted so we can't poison any of them (tonight anyway). Anyhow, I now have to get ready. More writing later.

* * *

Later

I think I danced with the Captain of the Guard. He fit the bill alright, tall, strong, terrible dancer. Couldn't do a waltz to save his life. I have no clue how one would survive a single battle without some dancing skills. It's the one part of Laitmean culture that I understand, fancy footwork to keep your enemies confused. Sadly, he did not give away any information that I could use. Even Sadderly, he really seemed to like me (who could blame him, I am charming). But that just makes him easier to kill or blackmail later. Trill was the lucky one. She danced with Prince Dowlin. THE PRINCE. He *likes* her. And even better, he is a pacifist. He says that when he becomes king, he is going to end this war, and set the borders with Haputa and not bother us.

226

Also, he basically gave the go ahead for us to kill his father. I like him. Even better, Lara was bored out of her skull at the ball. She got stuck dancing with some ancient nobleman. Shame she couldn't have danced with Prince Donis. he's just perfect for her. Rich and snobby to the last.

The Thief

91st day of fall

We did it!!! Quip and I entered the ballroom in wonderful disguises. We have been working on our speech so we don't have Haputian accents. (It was harder for Quip because she grew up on a farm before her parents died. My family was upper class and lived closer to the border, so I could switch to either accent.) Anyway, I wore navy and Quip wore red. Quip somehow snuck five-inch heels into my wardrobe, so I found myself constantly tottering. It was even worse when the dancing started.

Quip was stuck with a boring nobleman, no, I think he was the Captain of the Guards, and I danced with a boring noble. Until, what do you know, I found myself asked to dance by the Prince himself! I thought it was the second prince, Donis. But presently he introduced himself as Dowlin, the Crown Prince. (Even better!) He danced with me a lot and Quip caught on, sending me sly looks or funny faces, trying to make me laugh during the slower dances. I ignored her.

The Prince was constantly asking me questions, trying to unmask me. I answered his prying with the vaguest of answers, probably just egging him on. He eventually narrowed me down to either Lara, Quip, or, well, me. After a few minutes,He did figure out who I was, but of course he only knew me by my fake name. I guess I forgot to mention our fake names. Quip and I couldn't have our names because they're too Haputian, so Lara dubbed Quip

Evayah and me Addmaleta. I wonder if the Prince was a little suspicious about my identity? I brushed by that thought and let the conversation go where it would.

"The king's life has been threatened countless times and I now know of many poisons." He listed a few, but the one I really was interested in was listed a little later. "And then there's the Leavarus Vine. It can kill so quickly, that one doesn't know they're poisoned until they're dead. It makes it seem as though one's heart has stopped. Unusually, it is often found in gardens on the city's east side."

I sat up straight but quickly remembered not to act so interested. I wonder if he knows Lara's house is on the east side?

"What is this Leavarus Vine?" I asked cautiously. I had never heard of such a leaf.

"Oh, it's a skinny leaf that has points all on the edges. It usually grows somewhere towards the base of trees in the forests."

I changed the subject after that so I wouldn't seem so suspicious. But even though we talked about other things, ideas about the leaf were still circling in my head.

Dowlin stared curiously at me when I started to look off into the distance.

I must admit, Laitmean Princes are very handsome, with dark hair and intense brown eyes. My heart beat unusually fast which was very confusing. I kept the topic going about something like when the nearest merchant carts come again. I honestly don't remember our whole conversations. It all went by in a blur.

Suddenly, Ettalara was at my side tugging at my sleeve saying we had to go. A little disappointed, I made my excuses and left.

Whew! My feet hurt like I've pounded them with my truncheon! Good-night!

Redgenold

91st of fall, year 111

Quip. I don't quite know what I think meeting her again. All the old passion comes flooding back, but I try to temper it with the knowledge I have gained these past weeks- but I have not explained. Dowlin was practicing his dance steps in the hall when I came in. The first carriage was just coming up the drive, and the king was at the front with Guards and Dignitaries, leaving the servants, Dowlin, Donis, and I , and a few nervous Generals to pace the ballroom. I was going to ask Dowlin a thing or two about the invasion of Haputa, but then the doors were opened, and the people came flooding in. There are rules to a masked ball, but most all the guests were young and eager, so it soon descended into glorious chaos, everyone dancing with everyone else. It was all grand fun. I saw Arabell looking for me, and dodged her, as the next dance was a quick one, and she is awful at quick steps. I turned and bumped into one of the ladies who had recently entered town, with the girl called Ettalara. I knew they were called Evayah and Addmaleta, and had not spoken to either. But when the music started, I found myself beside her, and knew at once that it was Quip- not Evayah. She was in a red ball gown, with a flame mask, speaking and dancing like a lady, but I would have recognized her anywhere. Quip! She did not know me, or if she did, she hid it well. We were together for two quick dances, and one slow. In the end I did not want to let go of her, but I did. I danced with a few other girls, but did not even try to guess their names. I saw Dowlin dancing with a girl that might have been Trill, made unrecognizable with a midnight blue dress and her hair in long ringlets- whoever she was, Dowlin wouldn't release her hand and they laughed and talked for a long time. I danced with Quip again, still in such a daze, I think I stepped on her foot. In the end I staggered, drunk, truly drunk, not pretending, onto a balcony to watch the stars spin. I woke there this morning, with a pounding headache, and the pattern of the balcony rail pressed across my cheek. For all that I promised myself not to go to pieces when next I saw her, I cannot help it- I love her more than ever.

The Lady

91st day of fall

That was the most tedious party I have ever attended! At dinner I was seated next to a plump woman on my left and an old man with hearing problems on my right. She never stopped talking, even when there was food in her mouth, and he kept saying "eh?" so that she had to repeat herself even louder. As a result, I was half deaf by the end of the meal and about ready to scream from frustration.

The dancing was worse. Evayah and Addmaleta got decent partners, but I was stuck with all the old gentlemen who stepped on my toes, young boys who danced like wild horses, or rich nobles who thought they were being clever, when in fact they were just broadcasting their dullness. The girls teased me about it all the way home. I would say they've certainly gotten even with me for all my nagging the other night.

At The Masked Ball

The Thief

4th day of winter

Posture, horsemanship, eating, walking, sleeping, talking, moving. Lara makes me feel like a wound up toy that's at her disposal. But one that might spin out of control at any minute.

The Warrior

Year 111, 4th day of winter

We convinced Lara to hold a party of her own so we can do a little more snooping. Then we will, Trill will that is, call Dart to us, and send Haputa the information before we kill the king.

Yes, you heard right. Lara's garden is full of Dowlin's mystery plant, which I must find a way to sneak into the palace. I shall formulate a plan post party. Whoopee! So now I just have to make sure that the Captain of the Guard is not on the guest list. Knowing Lara, she'll invite him anyway, but it's worth a shot.

The Lady

5th Day of Winter

Evayah and Addmaleta had so much fun at the masquerade, that they have convinced me to host a ball! Of course, they want to "help." Addmaleta insisted on putting together the dinner menu (which consisted mainly of desserts) and Evayah wanted to write the invitations! I asked her if she knew calligraphy and she asked if it was anything like cursive. That's when I knew I must intervene. I helped Addmaleta revise her menu (she was none too happy about it). I told Evayah she could write the guest list and I would write the invitations. She said that was fine, but when I got the list, I found she had invited all the boring nobles and "forgotten" the Captain of the Guard.

I revised the list, sent out the invitations and went down to the kitchen. Somehow, Addmaleta had snuck acorn squash (my least favorite food) on the menu, so I took it off again and told the cook to disregard any demands to the contrary.

The Thief

5th day of winter

Success!!! Quip and I have convinced Lara to throw a ball at our mansion. She was skeptical at first, but we said we'd help so she finally said yes. Quip is enthusiastically writing the invitations. She got in trouble when Lara found out she didn't know how to write in calligraphy and 'forgot' to invite the Captain of the Guard, who she claims is boring. I don't know if that's true. He was very handsome and knew how to converse excellently. I was in charge of the dinner menu. Remembering the masquerade ball, I didn't want to serve all the same boring food, so I put things on it that everyone loves. No main courses or appetizers on this menu! It's all desserts!!! Lara was furious and was especially put out that I stuck acorn squash, with icing on top, on the menu. She snatched my task away from me and did it herself. She made me go upstairs and pick out the shoes I wanted, which is a pretty dull thing to do. Quip had already chosen a red pair with little jewels and sparkles on them that make my thief's hand burn trying not to touch.

Lara just came back and said I could choose only three desserts for the menu. Seeing acorn squash off it, I ordered the cook to put it back on. She said Lara had told her to leave it off and I was tempted to threaten her with my truncheon but remembered just in time that I was supposed to be a Lady so I refrained. Instead, I convinced her to put it back on using a few coins I had collected. (It's amazing what people will do for money!)

* * *

6th day of winter

Ettalara and her servants came today to fit me for my dress. It's tedious and boring. But, I do like what they chose. It will be blue (Again!) but will fade from light nearly white blue, at the top of the dress, to a dark blue by the bottom hem of the dress.

Redgenold

9th of Winter, year 111

A disturbing thought has entered my mind. Quip and Trill have, through unknown means that most likely involve Ettalara, gained quick entry to Laitmean society. That itself is not odd- I did a similar thing *without* Ettalara, but I do wonder- Quip knows me only as Captain of the Guard, Trill knows Dowlin only as Prince, and they made a point to dance with us, at a time when we would not know them. They are clearly spying, perhaps planning to bring Laitmea down- But that is what Dowlin wants. He deliberately put in place a Haputian Captain of the Guard, and is now handing Trill whatever she wants on a silver platter. The two are well suited to each other, I think. Dowlin wants to bring his father down. His every action is calculated to give Haputa the upper hand, in hopes that it will end the king's reign. I suspect the rumors of Darin's killing his own wife are not apocryphal as I once thought. It is the only explanation for Dowlin's willingness to turn on him. Vengeance for his mother, yes, but he also may have inherited the insanity that drives people to be murders. I do not think he would mind terribly much if Quip and Trill assassinated king Darin, really. He's playing us to get the throne. I don't doubt that he would do right by Haputa, and all countries, but nonetheless, I regret stepping into the mire that is Laitmean politics. Dowlin scares me.

* * *

10th of Winter, year 111

A party is being held at Ettalara's residence. I shall go, if only to see Quip. I passed the invitation on to Dowlin, who smiled and said something about "That charming Addmaleta girl" funny that he falls in love with a girl who is as like as not plotting his father's death. But then, so is he. Donis just grumbled when Dowlin announced that they were going. In Haputa, they say Darin killed his older brother to take the throne. Again, I thought it to be a tall tale cooked up by the likes of Quip, to rally us all against our foe, but after having spoken to the king on several occasions now, I begin to wonder if it is not all true. There is something quite *off* about him, hard to name exactly, but a kind of cold callousness that is even more disturbing than Dowlin's manipulative theatrics. The Prince, at least, uses violence as a means to an end.

The Thief

15th day of winter

Today is the ball! Quip has decided that we must write a quick message to Haputa to tell them about the Court, the Princes, and the strange poison Dowlin told me about. I'm trying to be as brief as I can but it's hard when the paper is so small. I'll talk about the ball later; right now I need to focus.

The Warrior

Year 111, 15th day of winter

So the prince, Dowlin, that is, has invited himself over. He really likes Trill. And Donis isn't too afraid of Lara either. But the captain of the guard is REDGE. Ug. How in Eretz did he get here? And how can I make him go back?

17

i

The Man

rest never, toil on,

ever labor, never rest,

do not stop if hope is gone,

give your all, do your best.

even when you do it all,

no thanks you will receive,

only, though it galls,

loving her is your reprieve.

does she know you love her?

i think not.

17

ii

16 The Beast

loyal, sweet and kind,

over fields she does plod,

verily, no better friend shall you find.

ever plowing up the land, leave unturned no clod.

yet when her master falls behind,

on she goes before,
unless he calls she shall not stop 'til all the fields are lined.

iii
The Land
turn me over
run me through
under plant, then weed the clover
let me grow anew.
yearly I will thaw and freeze
I change slowly,
don't you see?
only a fool would call me lowly.

Redgenold

15th of Winter, year 111

Today is the party. I shall see Quip again- and this time not go to pieces!

* * *

Later

I do not even know where to begin. I expected that Dowlin would ask for Trill's hand, but after a normal, straight forward party- not the mess that was today. Quip recognized me without my mask, and it became clear that I would not get another chance with her. I was desperate to show her how I've changed, so when she left, I followed. Well perhaps I haven't changed enough. I didn't notice that she followed Trill, or that Dowlin followed me, until Quip rounded on me and attacked. Trill was probably sending secret information back to Haputa. Dowlin tried to break Quip and me apart, but she had me in a headlock, and was shouting obscenities at the moon. For a moment, I wondered why I love her so, but then she released me, and my head hit a rock so hard it hurt too much for me to wonder anymore. When I stopped seeing stars, Donis had come upon us, dragging Ettalara behind him like she was a disobedient puppy. He had us jammed into his carriage, and was just untying the horses from their post, when I remembered the first time I had seen Quip, just after she'd lost her family.

I had wanted to comfort her- to hold her hand and tell her it would end all right, but hadn't known how to say it. I'd gotten her out of the corner in the end, but the guilt I'd felt for how I'd done it, tormenting the little boy, had never truly left me. I felt like my skin was two sizes too small, surely I would burst into a thousand pieces, and I could feel a goose egg sized lump forming on the top of my head. Somehow I blurted out "I love you" and Quip went mad. She's always been like that- to lose one's parents so young messes with the mind. I know how it feels, but I never wanted it for her. I wanted the madness to leave her for good, to always see the real Quip who is so kind and so loyal.

I wished- I do not know what I wished. By then we were bundled into the throne room, and Donis was speaking, and Quip had picked some spiky little leaves on our forced march back to the carriage, how Donis didn't notice I don't know, but she was chewing them all the same.

It was all a blur around her, as she slipped the leaves into the king's cup of wine.

"I love you!" I shouted it that time, for who knows what reason. All I knew was that I had failed to comfort the little girl in the corner, I had failed to help her when we were taken for slaves, I had failed to stay by her in the boat, I had failed to hold her hand for the last slow dance- but whatever happened, I would not let her slip away now. When she came at me I could see that she was flagging- there were a few glancing blows, I tried to hold her as I would in a dance and she backpedaled, our momentum sending her into the empty throne.

Empty because king Darin had collapsed dead on the floor. Dowlin had his fathers' crown on askew, and had Trill in his arms- to my astonishment, she didn't seem to mind. Normally she flees from hugs. They'll make a fine couple. Ettalara and Donis both seemed rather put out- though I doubt Donis' tears were for his father. Quip was taken back to her room ill from poison, and a doctor sent in to tend to her, and when the lump on my head was discovered, I too was sent away.

In conclusion, Darin certainly got his just deserts, but I do not know what is between me and Quip now, or how she will see my confession once she is recovered.

I'll go to bed now, as my head still throbs.

8

100 101 The Iceman
The turn of a cart wheel,
the jingle of bells,
some ribbon, a banner,
oh heavenly smells!
A vendor with meat,
a vendor with cheese,
a merchant with cold-cure
-but didn't he sneeze?
Laughter and shouting,
there's a festival here,
-Look at the jester!
it's that time of year.
The cavalry came,
their horses all prancing,
and out in the streets
the people are dancing.
Come look!
Come see!
Come buy
from me!

Come see the attractions,
juggler, magician, the man who swallows his lance,
the famed fire-eater,
oh watch the flames dance!
But the best booth around,
in the heat of the day,
the iceman, that vendor
down queen's Way.
A crown and five,
to watch that wheel churn,
the wondrous sweet cream
for which we all yearn.
The line stretches so far,
its end a mile away,
there's no doubt at all,
He's got good business today.
A crown and five,
for a dish of your own,
then go on your way,
so happily home.
But by his horse stands a girl,
she hasn't a penny,
no matter how nice,
for her there's not any.
She asked oh so sweetly,
but none would he give,
she tried to take some,
(for without ice cream how would one live?)
When I reach the front,
I'll buy not one but two.
One for me, one for her,
oh Iceman, none for you.

The Thief

~⚬⚬⚬~

15th day of winter

Well…. This is an interesting turn of events.

The ball went fine until Quip and I decided that we should send the message to the Senate. I slipped out first with Quip guarding my back. We headed for the gardens, which were surrounded by a nice ring of trees. I called Dart and he flew quickly to my side, his powerful wings rustling the branches around us. I extracted the note from my pocket only to hear footsteps. Redge, Captain of the Guard, had followed us! Not only had he turned coat and become Laitmean, he was trying to capture us! Quip must have missed him or something because she should have seen him, being the rear guard. Anyhow, he jumped out, barely gave me a glance, and went for Quip. She was furious and I don't think the entire Haputian army could have stopped her as she whipped out her knife, which glinted wickedly in the moonlight, and attacked Redge with all her fury. To his credit, he held up a lot better than I thought he would and lasted a good two minutes or so before looking tired. Then, as I was turning back to stick my letter into Dart's mouth, another voice startled us. Dowlin! Quip was very sloppy that night if she had missed *two* people! I felt horrible for Dowlin to find out now that I was working for his enemy. I really did enjoy being with him and this wasn't how I imagined the end of our relationship. But to my shock, he seemed to suddenly be siding with Quip in the fight and managed to separate the two. After a struggle, for Quip

250

was very hard to separate, he turned to ask me what exactly was going on, but to everyone's horror, Donis showed up dragging Lara along with him. Lara looked so shocked I had to resist the urge to laugh. Donis, on the other hand, was furious. He demanded that we all follow him to see his father or he would call the guards.

He made us all get in a carriage and then carried us off to the palace. On the way there, Redge suddenly burst out and said that he was in love with Quip! He must have hit his head, the poor boy. Then I remembered how much he had stuck close to Quip at the masked ball, and at the slave training camp, and at, well, everywhere. So that explains a lot. Quip didn't take it so well, which is to say she tried to attack him.

By the time we got Quip under control, we were being herded into the throne room by the still livid younger Prince. The king of Laitmea looked up lazily as we entered. He was not as fat or unobservant as I thought he might be. Actually he was kind of lanky, with cold calculating blue eyes and black hair. His only fault (besides being a ruthless dictator), was overconfidence.

He questioned each of us harshly when Donis had explained where he found us. Lara foolishly denied knowing who we really are. Before, I might have been angry, but since it was out of self preservation and not a desire to betray us, I let it slide. I'm pretty sure the king thought she was lying anyway.

Uneasily, I watched Quip sneak up to the king's throne, (there were no guards in sight surprisingly) and drop a green, mushy, slightly drippy, clump of chewed stuff into the king's drink. I held my breath. Could she really have stuck the poison in there that easily? Would the king notice the poison and have us beheaded? Would we be beheaded after he drank it for killing the king? Fortunately, Quip proved to be a sufficient diversion as she attacked Redge, who caught her and said he loved her. Again. Honestly, that boy is like a lovesick puppy! I hope Quip does marry him just so he can move on with his life and stop bothering the rest of us. He needs to work on holding his tongue.

The king motioned his guards, alright, so there were a few, to break up the fight just as he took a sip of his drink. Less than a minute later, he was slumped over in his chair. Dead. I could have danced for joy. It was all over!

After everything we've been through, the king was as dead as a door-nail! (And a rusty one at that.)

Dowlin rushed over to his father, felt his pulse (or lack thereof), and officially declared him dead. Then he took the crown from his father's head and placed it on his own.

"He won't be needing that anymore," he muttered. He ordered his father's body to be removed from the room. The guards complied eagerly and I caught tears of joy running down some of their faces.

Suddenly, Quip was falling into the empty throne, breathing heavily. Redge stood in the corner looking shocked. For the first time in his life, he had beaten Quip! I was impressed but worried how she would take it. So Quip was not invincible after all!

Lara must have slipped out sometime after this, but I don't really remember clearly, because the next thing I knew, Dowlin got down on his knee in front of me. Pulling out his mother's ring from his pocket, he said,

"Addmaleta, I've loved you since I first set eyes on you. Will you do me the honor of becoming my wife?" He looked up at me, his warm brown eyes shining with hope. But I looked away with tears in my own.

"Dowlin, I haven't been straight with you," I whispered, wiping the ridiculously emotional tears off my cheeks, "my name isn't Addmaleta, it's Trill. I'm an orphan and a thief from Haputa. I'm not worthy of becoming your wife." I started to turn away from him, but he caught my hand.

"Trill," he said, his eyes glistening even more than mine, "None of that matters to me. You are beautiful, smart, brave and, most importantly, kind. You are not afraid to do what's right even when it's hard. I can't think of anyone I'd rather spend my life with than you." Then he stood up and kissed me.

I was shocked. Me! The Haputian thief, kissing the new king of Laitmea! But I didn't pull away. In fact, I almost unconsciously picked his pocket before remembering not to.

Finally, he drew back and offered the ring again. To think, he was meaning to do this all along, and still went through with it after finding out that I was working for Haputa! This time, I accepted it, and not just for how expensive it looked. I wasn't even thinking about how much it was worth to sell it! With that, the most strange and yet most beautiful evening of my life ended.

The Lady

꒰ ꒱

15th Day of Winter

The party seemed to be going well. The dinner was a great success (even
though acorn squash somehow made it back on the menu). Prince Dowlin
and Prince Donis surprised us by showing up, and so naturally everyone was
on their best behavior. Dowlin and Addmaleta seemed to enjoy each other's
company which surprised me. Apparently, they met at the last ball, but I was
so busy trying not to get my toes stepped on I didn't notice.

The Captain of the Guards seemed rather enamored by Evayah (which
explains why she "forgot" to put his name on the guest list) and stuck close
to her through the whole evening. Even I got to have a lengthy conversation
with Prince Donis! He is quite an eloquent speaker, and I rather enjoyed his
company.

Everything was going well and I began to hope we might get through an
entire evening without any mishaps. That is, until about half way through
the evening when I saw Addmaleta slip out. I didn't think anything of it
until Evayah snuck out too, followed by the Captain of the Guard shortly
thereafter. Then Prince Dowlin followed them and I really got suspicious. I
excused myself from Donis and hurried after them.

I followed them all the way past the garden to a small grove of trees. Ducking
behind one, I surveyed the strange scene in front of me.

Trill (there's no point in writing their fake names anymore) was sending

Dart the dragon back into the sky (I suppose with top secret information intended for Haputa) and Quip was battling the Captain of the Guards who had evidently turned out to be none other than Redge! I shall refrain from speculating as to how that happened. Suddenly Prince Dowlin strode forward and put a stop to their fight.

He asked them what they were doing. They answered him, and though I couldn't quite make out what they were saying, I think the Prince got a pretty clear idea of what was going on.

I thought that certainly he would haul them all off to prison to be beheaded, but the prince seemed to have other ideas. He was settling the fight in Quip and Trill's favor!

Thinking that all was well, I turned to make my way back to the party, only to come face to face with Donis!

"Come on," he said, and without waiting for me, marched right up to the assembled group. I followed mutely.

The younger Prince made a very long speech about how shocking these developments were and how upset he was that his brother seemed to be helping spies, but the long and the short of it is, he stuck all of us in a carriage (which he drove himself) and took us directly to the king himself!

As if this were not crazy enough, while we were in the carriage, Redge professed his love for Quip! Quip lunged at him, and it took everyone else in the carriage to hold her back.

Finally, we arrived at the palace. We were taken straight to the king, who is not as handsome as he looks in his portrait. Donis gave a complete explanation and the king interrogated each of us. I had to deny knowing who Quip and Trill really were to protect myself, but I'm not sure the king believed me. I am not very good at coming up with false explanations on the spot.

Quip, meanwhile, was edging closer and closer to the king. A moment later, she discreetly took a disgusting lump of chewed greens out of her mouth and plopped them in the king's drink. A month earlier I would have called her out on it right away, but seeing as we would probably wind up in prison (or worse) if the king lived, I did not object.

The next few minutes were utter confusion. The king took a sip of his

255

drink, Quip attacked Redge (for again professing his love) and everybody started shouting at everybody else so that it took a while before we realized the king had keeled over and died.

In the chaos that followed, Dowlin pronounced his father dead, took the crown, and proposed to Trill (who said yes), Donis threw a temper tantrum because he couldn't be king, and (best of all) REDGE BEAT QUIP!!!!! She fell onto the now empty throne bruised and panting and looking quite ill, though whether that was from chewing the poison or the mortification of being bested by her enemy-turned-love I could not say. For my part, I slipped quietly away, walked home, and went to bed.

I Find Your Countenance Displeasing

Your looks leave much to be desired
Surely you're not the one they hired
To clear my table scraps away?
Well I won't have you one more day.
This mongrel is for hunting are you sure?
He looks to me like he's a cur.
Find a new one on the double
Hurry or you'll be in trouble.
The dignitary so and so
Told me where I ought to go.
Well I won't have it any more.
Feel free to hang him, this is war!
And what's the matter with the cook?
She doesn't have it in her book?
Then fire her and find another!
I want squid meat for my supper.
No, silk pajamas just won't do
I only ask the best of you.
Give me what I want right now,
And don't forget you have to bow!
Don't tell me I'm king I already know.

What do you call this circus show?
This isn't service, it's a joke,
Have your dinner. I hope you choke.
What do you mean, "the people hate me"?
They just have poor taste, you see,
I'm the best they've ever had!
Oh, forget about my dad!

The Warrior

Year 111, 16th day of winter

Redgenold loves me. I think I shall vomit.

Better now.

Trill left the party to call Dart, and I followed for a rear guard, and also so I could pick a few leaves from that rather interesting vine Trill had told me about.

Redge followed me, so I had to fend him off, until Dowlin came in to break up the fight, (and probably sweep Trill off her feet and declare his undying love to her, but he never got the chance) and all was fine, until who should come in but Donis and Lara. And Donis is just about the biggest Laitmean ever. So he declares Trill and I spies, and calls his big brother and Lara helpers, and carts us all off to his father, Wrinkle Face his Smelliness, king of Laitmayonnaise. (and Lara doesn't like my insults). And on the way there Redge declares his love for me. Aaaaaaaargh. When we got to the palace, the king, was in the middle of supper. I was chewing on some leaves at the time, (just to see if they taste good, don't want to kill the king with substandard vegetables. It also helped release the poison so he could drink it. I think he might've noticed if there were chewy bits.) They were a nice consistency by the time I got close enough to get them into the kings cup without him noticing. Apparently he died swiftly of heart failure, (The official death announcement says so,) but I never saw that, because I attacked Redge. What can I say? Love hurts.

But Redge beat me. It had to have been the little bit of poison I swallowed, because I do not remember Redge being that strong. Or that smart. I went flying, and ended up on the now empty throne. Before I blacked out, I saw Dowlin take the crown, with a (rather fake) tear in his eye, and then ask Trill to be the queen. Donis went off to throw a temper tantrum. I was then carted away to vomit in peace. It might have been the poison, it might have been Redge.

KING DARIN

The Lady

⁂

16th Day of Winter

When I woke up this morning, I thought at first that the events of last night were but a dream. However when I saw the time and realized I had overslept for the first time since my parents died, I realized that it had been all too real.

I feel so strange. Everything happened so fast that I hardly know what to think. King Darin is dead and Prince Dowlin shall be crowned king soon, I should imagine. He and Trill are to be wed, as well, before the coronation. Who would have thought that Trill, the thief, the orphan, the fighter, the loyal Haputian, would become queen of Laitmea? I did have a little talk with Trill this afternoon. I was asking her how she was feeling about her new role as queen Regent once she marries Dowlin, and she admitted that she is a little nervous. I did find out, however, that Trill was once quite wealthy herself. Haputa doesn't have nobility, but if they did, Trill's parents would be something like Count and Countess. That explains a few things. From a glance, Trill may appear to be a common thief (indeed, that is what I thought when I first met her) but when one gets to know her, there are little things, hard to put a finger on, that set her apart. Things do have a funny way of turning out exactly how I least expected them to.

Quip is recovering in the bedchamber of our temporary home for the time being. The poison she held in her mouth, while not enough to kill her, made her violently ill. At first I thought she was playing up her condition for the fun of it, but we called a doctor, and he said that she needs to remain in bed for the foreseeable future. She's a strong person, but has sustained so much abuse in her short life that I doubt she'll ever be fully right again.

I intend to see Donis about getting my own home back. I am willing to pay for it; there's more than enough money in the treasure stash, but without royal intervention I don't see how I'll be able to convince whosoever is living there that it is rightfully mine.

The Thief

16th Day of Winter

Apparently, once I wed Dowlin, I shall become queen Regent. That means Dowlin and I are in charge even though we weren't officially crowned. Dowlin came to visit me today and said that the peace talks are to begin tomorrow and he wants me there. I am a little nervous but didn't show it, and he said I would do fine. He especially wants me there when the Haputian senators arrive so that I can try to come up with a solution that both countries will like. I said sure (hopefully I won't get too bored) and my thief's brain immediately calculated how many trinkets, buttons, hair decorations, and adornments I could steal. Dowlin thanked me and left. I realized only after he had gone that I had taken his gold watch. Curses!!! It had to be returned immediately, and so I called him back in, told him I loved him, kissed him, and slipped it back into his pocket. Whew! Crisis averted!!!

The Warrior

Year 111,17th day of winter

So Redge loves me. I know I keep writing it, but it still astounds me. As long as I've known him, he's been a bully, and seemed to want to provoke me. That he did it all just to get my attention is mind-blowing. I've not talked with him much since that disaster of a party, and I've only hit him once. Lara keeps saying that it'd be poetic justice if I married him, but I'm not so sure. I threatened to feed her to Dart the last time she said it, and that shut her up for a good five seconds. Aaaaaaaargh. Right now I just want this stupid war to be over so I can shout my head off in peace.

The Tantrum

The baby of the family,
oh how he does scream and shout.
And when he does not get all he wants,
he throws his toys about.
His family was in distress,
His father tried to be stern.
"No tantrums!"
but would the boy learn?
His mother was kinder,
"Dear, this isn't right."
but her gentleness wouldn't dissuade him.
He continued to scream with all of his might.
His aunts and uncles,
why, they simply caved.
He got what e'er he wanted.
And so the way was paved.
When he wanted a tiger,
a tiger there'd be,
right here, right now!
for all to see.
What a magnificent beast,

all orange and black.
it's said for noise-making
he's got a knack.
"let's hear a roar"
the boy did say,
"This instant! This moment!
for heaven's sake, today!"
Nothing.
How he shouted,
how he screamed,
oh, how he pouted.
Nothing.
At last the tiger did oblige,
and opened his mouth,
so slowly, so wide!
But no sound came out.
Was something wrong?
One little growl-
it couldn't possibly take this long!
How strange.
Perhaps something was blocking the noise?
He promptly stood up,
then tripped on his toys.
How gracefully he fell,
none heard him scream,
and the tiger's jaws closed,
with him in between.

The Lady

17th Day of Winter

When I knocked on Donis' door this afternoon, I was not prepared for the state in which I would find him and his room. Feathers from pillows were strewn all over and there were shards of broken glass on the floor. Paintings and tapestries hung askew and books had been pulled from the shelves. The prince was sitting sulkily in the only upright chair, arms folded across his chest.

"What do you want?" he asked grumpily.

At this, something inside me snapped. "Sir, is this any way to address a Lady?" I asked.

"No, and I don't particularly care," he grumbled, "what do you want me to do, ring for tea and crumpets and invite you in for a long chat?"

"That would be nice," I replied.

"And what is there to talk about?" Donis whined, his voice rising. "About how my father is dead? About how my brother stole the throne for himself and is now betrothed to a peasant girl?"

"Well for one thing, complaining isn't going to help anything," I snapped, "and as to your brother 'stealing' the throne, it was his rightfully, simply because he was born first. That's nobody's fault and griping about it isn't going to change a thing. And finally, for your information, Trill is not a peasant. She may have pretended to be one to blend in, but she never truly became one. She was born into a wealthy family, and though her father squandered that wealth, that doesn't change a thing. Yes, she stole things (and yes, that's wrong), but her character never changed. She was and is the nicest and noblest one of us all and I can't think of anyone better to become Laitmea's queen."

Donis stared at me after this outburst, shocked. I merely turned on my heels and marched away. I paused at the door, "By the way, the manner in which you behave when you don't get what you want is absolutely disgraceful. Next time I come in here (*if* I visit you again) I expect to see things cleaned up and I expect you to behave like a gentleman." With that I stalked away.

The Thief

17th Day of Winter

The expression on the Haputian Senator's faces when they walked in and saw me sitting next to Dowlin in all my finery was priceless. I was tempted to laugh at their wide eyes and gaping mouths.

Instead, I simply smiled craftily and tried to look like I wasn't gloating.

"You?!" one exclaimed. (I think he was the one who interrogated us back during the siege.) he wore a dark purple and brown robe, an overly large ruby ring, and his thin, balding hair was slicked back.

"Of course it's me!" I exclaimed, but definitely more regally than I would have said it before, as he knelt to kiss my hand. "Who else were you expecting?"

"But you're so…different than when I last saw you," he said with a shake of his head.

"Not quite so different as you might think," I smiled rather smugly as I handed him back his ruby ring. He stared agog for a second before regaining his composure. Behind me, Quip was snickering. Dowlin pretended not to notice.

The talks today went well and I think we have come to a reasonable agreement. Laitmea will return Haputa's land along with money and building supplies to help restore the country. Also, any people taken as slaves or forced to serve in Laitmea's army are to be returned, along with money to restart their lives in Haputa.

The Senators warned me that although some Haputians would be glad I was becoming Laitmea's queen, others might see it as betrayal. They told me that things may not go smoothly right away and that I will have to earn people's trust, Laitmeans and Haputians alike. That will be quite a task, as Haputians are naturally very suspicious people and do not treat traitors well.

I wasn't very satisfied by this final report and, when they left, nearly slouched in my chair. However, I was saved by this near failure in posture, by Quip who snorted rudely in the Haputians wake. Leave it to Quip to save the moment.

The Lady

18th Day of Winter

As I was dressing for the day, a knock came at my door. I made myself presentable and went to see who it was. A servant from the palace stood there with two letters addressed to me. I took them, thanked and dismissed the servant, and sat on my bed to read them.

The first was from Trill. It was a note on how well the peace talks are going. She's planning to meet with the Haputian Senators this afternoon and the Ambassador from Styllyg will be arriving in a few days. Haputa, Styllyg, and Onkay are to be given back all their land as well as money to make up for any damage.

The second letter surprised me. It was an apology from Donis for the way he behaved yesterday. He invited me over this afternoon for a walk in his private garden as he said his room is still being cleaned up. (I think he should clean it up himself, but I'll take that up with him later.) Anyway, I accepted his invitation and I'm meeting him in half an hour. I'd better go.

The Warrior

Year 111, 23rd day of winter

I'll admit that Redge is good looking, but no more. My feelings are honestly a bit of a jumble right now. Trill advised that I should write down everything I'm feeling and see if it helps, I'm a little skeptical, but I'll try.

First, I'm shocked about Redge liking me. He thinks he was obvious, but apparently I am very bad at reading young men, because I thought he hated me. I'm conflicted, because I've hated Redge for years, but he's like a different person now, all nice and civil-like. He's the sort of boy I'd envision myself marrying, but I'm not sure if I can put aside my feelings about the old Redge enough to love him. I'm also really frustrated with life, and not just my love life, (or what will be my love life if I decide to fall in love). I wanted to return to Haputa days ago, but there is still work to be done here. The war is not over yet, and there are all kinds of nobles and diplomats here in the Capitol to agree on the terms of Laitmea's surrender. I understand none of it, but Trill wants me here, so I'll stay. I must say, she's come into her own with this whole episode. She and Dowlin blather on about this and that and who will be Czar of Onkay next. They seem rather in love, which is good, as they are to be wed in a few weeks. The official Coronation will be on the following morning. They're just king and queen regent now, whatever that means. They seem to be in full power to me. Did I mention that I still don't like corsets?

Well, that's how I feel. Angry and frustrated and confused. And this whole writing about it thing has done no good whatsoever. I'm still convinced that screaming at the top of my lungs is the best way to deal with emotions. Now, on to the throwing knives.

* * *

Year 111,30th day of winter

Laitmea is not getting quite the death I wanted in previous rants, even the plague is not so bad now, but it is strange how things seem a little different. I know I have not been writing my mandatory once a week, but there is so much going on, and I doubt Trill even remembers our bet.

The Lady

32 Day of Winter

I haven't written in a while, but not much has happened. Trill and Dowlin are still negotiating with the other countries, which proved to be a bit more difficult than expected as half of Haputa is ecstatic that Trill is to be queen of Laitmea while the other half considers her a turncoat. Trill is working especially hard at pacifying her country to avoid civil war.

Quip is still resting. I don't think it's completely voluntary, though. I visited her yesterday, but she was feeling rather cranky and so I left early. Interestingly enough, besides Trill, Redge is the only one Quip will let stay with her. Sometimes he reads to her and once he even tried singing, but she punched him in the nose for that so he doesn't sing anymore. Romance is in the air.

Speaking of romance, Donis and I have become very good friends. (Perhaps, even more than friends?) He has made it no secret that he loves me. I suppose I could marry him eventually, but he gets more and more mature the longer I keep my distance, so I think he shall have to wait.

The Thief

36th day of winter

Most of the time I spend with Dowlin is taken up with drafting treaties and planning for our coronation, and I must say he is one of the most intelligent boys I have ever met. Although perhaps I'm biased, as I have fallen in love with him. Just yesterday, he leaned over and kissed me on the cheek. I had half a mind to slap him like Quip no doubt would, but I restrained my hand. Actually, I heard myself giggle a little. I nearly slapped myself. What made me become one of those ridiculous noblewomen who giggle and bat their eyes? It's despicable!!! Imagine me, doing a silly thing like giggling about a boy! I'm not the only one who's, perhaps, getting a bit ridiculous. I was talking with Quip, and I'm almost beginning to think that she enjoys Redge's company.

Quip and Redge! The whole world has turned upside down! A Haputian thief is going to be queen of Laitmea, and Quip is sweet on Redge. Maybe they've both been hit on their heads a few to many times?

Anyway, I must be going.

The Warrior

Year 111,38th day of winter
  As Trill explains it, all countries who lost land to Laitmea now get it back, and they'll never be invaded again. Haputa shall indeed be forever.

The Lady

39th Day of Winter

There is to be a ball in a few weeks! Donis has asked me to go with him and so I shall. I'm going to wear a lovely lavender ball gown with long lavender gloves, lavender shoes, and lavender earrings. I think Quip is going with Redge, which shall be interesting to say the least. She claims she's not very excited, but I know better. As I passed her bedchamber this morning, I heard her fretting to Trill about what she should wear and how she should do her hair. Love does strange things to a person.

I have also discovered, largely due to Donis, that my father never had any debts. He and mother had managed their estate well, and upon their deaths, I ought to have received a modest inheritance in addition to the emergency funds and the house.

My father did, however, have a rather poor relationship with king Darin, who forced my fathers' lawyer to forge new documents giving all of the money directly to Darin. He wanted me in the service so that I would be out of his way and unable to press charges. The only reason he didn't take the hidden money was because my mother had kept it secret. Fortunately Darin was *not* so good at keeping secrets, and Donis uncovered all of the forgeries. With my own account of events, this should be sufficient to restore my property to me.

Redgenold

41st of Winter, year 111

Dowlin has sent word for the Laitmean army to prepare to withdraw its forces from outside the borders, and has called all the near nations to a peace conference, in which Laitmea will officially stand down. I shall be kept in charge of the army, though if he makes good on his promises, it will be a much smaller affair. The Haputian Senate, Onkay's Czar, the Prime Minister of Styllyg, and some officials from Mer have arrived in Lyrah, and peace talks finish tomorrow. Dowlin has asked me to attend, and guard him should the need arise. While most people are pleased with the proceedings, there are some who would have marched on Haputa come spring, and death to the man who stands in their way. They may cause some trouble before all is said and done.

The Thief

41st of winter

Dowlin has called Laitmea's army back to the capitol. I wonder how Redge feels about that?

I've been sitting at meetings, smiling like my face is permanently stuck that way all day, and I have to say that even after hiding my feelings all my life I'm still having trouble keeping up the mask in public. It's hardest of all to keep from laughing, for in addition to his good looks and intelligence, Dowlin has a great sense of humor. Quip was sitting behind me today, and set back proceedings two days by openly guffawing at the Prime Minister of Styllyg. He said something or other about missing a line in one of the treaties he was supposed to sign, honestly whatever he said floated out of my head the minute he was done talking, and Dowlin muttered that perhaps he had left it in the ice cream cart. (I had told him about Lara's Diary in private, you see.) I almost died trying to keep a straight face and had to stare fixedly at a portrait of one of the ancient, dusty kings hanging on the wall like it was the most interesting thing I'd ever seen. Honestly, why do they keep such ugly portraits in the throne room anyway? The king's offensive frown, thick, oily hair, and horrid fox teeth remind me too much of the headmistress at the orphanage.

I haven't actually heard much from Lara recently. I'm still staying with her and Quip, although I'll move into the palace soon enough, but she's been away almost as much as I have. Probably seeing Donis. I really don't understand how such a little snobbish nincompoop could be related to Dowlin. He's helping Lara get her house back. I'm sure he's struggling with all the work, having to sign his name on documents, multiple times. I think he's in love with Lara though. He must be, if he'll brave paper-cuts for her. It's funny that Quip has the run of the house most of the time. She's the least suited of all of us to be a noblewoman. I think she's been redecorating. I noticed a bunch of throwing knives stuck in the wall of the front entrance.

4

She always is obedient, she always follows the rules,
She always dresses handsomely, arrayed in gems and jewels.
Proper etiquette and grammar are the keys to her success,
For in Laitmean society, 'tis with these one is assessed.
She's loyal to her country and to all those she holds dear,
She only tries to do what's right though that path is fraught with fear.
But though she seems transparent, there's more than meets the eye,
Her life is filled with sadness, though to that she'd likely lie.
Alone in a troubled world and assigned a dangerous task,
She hides her grief and fear behind an ever-hardening mask.
Though she would insist she's fine, the only thing she really wants,
Is for someone to care enough for her to look beyond her taunts.
To see her as a human, and not as a pawn to be checked,
To treat her with compassion, kindness, and also with respect.
Until that day, though, do beware, for she is frightened and hurt,
Never underestimate a girl of noble birth.

31 The Lady

The Lady

43rd Day of Winter

Donis has insisted on paying for repairs to my house. He says he can have it ready for me to move in by the first day of spring! I'm so happy! If only I could marry him. I still feel it isn't quite time, but every day that passes I fall more and more in love. He really does have a beautiful smile. I must move back to my old house as soon as it is ready. If I stay here much longer, I'm liable to do something foolish. But oh, sometimes it's lovely to be young and foolish.

Redgenold

45th of Winter, year 111

Quip and I have been talking, more than we ever did in Haputa. A ball is to be held for the Foreign Dignitaries, and I shall ask her to go with me.

* * *

47th of Winter, year 111

It has gotten a little easier not to trip over my own feet in her presence, but every now and then that green eyed gaze renders me speechless. She'll dance with me, though I can't tell what her feelings are on the matter.

The Thief

47th day of winter

This takes the cake! Quip has agreed to dance with Redge!

There'll be a ball tomorrow night to mark the end of the war between Haputa and Laitmea. As the queen to be, I shall be dancing with Dowlin. (Just how we met! That first dance feels like ages ago.) I think I'll wear a new color of dress. Maybe sea green? It's Dowlin's favorite color. Goodness, his name comes up a lot in my past few entries! I love him almost as much as Ice cream. (And is it just me, or has vanilla only gotten better whenever I eat it?)

Lara is going with Donis, of course. How is it sickening when they're in love? Most people know how to be, well, not sickening. Lara says she's not ready to get married, and I have to agree.

The Warrior

Year 111,48th day of winter

There is a ball tonight. Redge has asked to go with me. I said yes, though I don't know why. Ettalara would never let me hear the end of it if I had a good time, so I will insist upon being miserable. I asked Trill, and she says that she and Dowlin may stop by after they are done talking to some important person or other from Styllyg.

* * *

Year 111,49th day of winter

Redge kissed me. ON THE MOUTH. We were dancing, and talking, and suddenly he just leaned in and did it. Who knows how long it took him to work up the courage to do that. As much as I hate him, it was fine. I hit him across the face for it, still, I do hope he'll try again. I suppose he needs to practice somchow. Ettalara has been remarkably civilized about it. Trill sure wasn't though. I told her to bugger off because she's the one getting wed next week, but she just snorted at me and stole my red feather hair pin. I don't know how she did it without me feeling it.

The Thief

49th of winter

Redge Kissed Quip! How hysterically poetic and wonderfully just things turned out. I have teased Quip mercilessly, though she did point out that I am going to get married soon, so I guess I should stop. But ah, what joy it brings me to finally have the upper hand over her. Other than the horror that is wedding planning, things have been rather boring. It seems like every time I step outside my room, a servant is there requesting I look over such and such, or that Lady so and so has come to visit. (A Lady that I never even heard of.) In short, I'm tired of all this planning. Maybe Dowlin would like to elope? We could use Dart as the getaway transportation and if the priest likes dragons and heights, he could marry us while we're riding! Wow! I like this idea! I don't think Dowlin would approve, though. (Quip might.) However, in the meantime, I have resorted to my old pastimes to avoid driving myself insane.

A list of things I have "borrowed" today:

Quips' Hair pin.

Dowlin's' least expensive ring- I gave it back.

Two Senators' cuff-links- I did not give them back.

Eight gold watches from various people who are better off without them.

A leather belt with a silver buckle- Dart has it now.

A gold candle wick trimmer with platinum inlay. Who needs that? I'm keeping it. Now I will retire to my bedchamber.

Redgenold

49th of winter, year 111

Oh, clumsy, clumsy me. I opened my mouth to speak, and found myself kissing her. She smells of cinnamon, and has eyes like an angry wolf. I got a slap for my efforts, but I think she was pleased.

The Thief

50th day of winter.

DEATH TO WHOEVER THOUGHT UP PETTICOATS! I swear I will murder them with their own invention!!! My wedding gown is going to be all white. AAAAAAAAAAAAAAAAAAAAAAAAAAAAAAAAAAAAAAAAAAAAAAAAA!

How can anyone wear all white? I personally like navy blue. The dark color hides blood stains very well. But white? Anything will show up. What if I have to take Dart out for a ride and bird poop gets on it? Or if I climb a tree and it tears? Quip would say 'who cares?' but Lara would murder me. No one likes my idea of having my dress resemble the ocean. I wanted it to be close fitting just until the waist line then flow freely with little sparkly crystals across the skirt, like water, down to the ground. I wanted it to have a mix of colors, all blue, that would really resemble the ocean and freedom. No one wants that, though. I have to wear this archaic dress that is tight, uncomfortable, fitted and has been passed down from queen to queen. BLAH! I'd rather wear a feed-sack.

＊

52nd of winter

More mishaps today.

I was trying to sneak out the window to escape more etiquette lessons

290

and wedding plans and was climbing down the tree outside my window. Unfortunately, my dress caught on a limb, curse these overbearing dresses, and I had to yank on it to escape being stuck there. I heard a rip, snap, before I tumbled down and face-planted in the mud. I had just sat up and wiped the muck off my face when I came face to face with the Haputian Senators. They were still shocked at my sudden entrance, as was I, but the one with the extra large ruby ring huffed, "you were right, you haven't changed."

I wanted to slap him, but I had to behave like a queen, no matter how awkward the situation.

"At least I don't change for the worse." Well, maybe it wasn't a queenly response. However, they frowned, bowed and walked off. I wondered how long they'll get in the day before noticing the ruby ring is gone.

Redgenold

54th of Winter, year 111

Trill and Dowlin are to be wed the day after next, and the whole palace is abuzz. It has been many years since queen Elisabet passed on- (I have learned that she was almost certainly killed, if not by Darin, at his order), so it shall be interesting to see how the place does with a new queen. She and Dowlin will be properly crowned afterwards, although Dowlin has been wearing the crown everywhere already. Once they are officially the monarchs of Laitmea, they can sign the necessary treaties and bring this cursed war to an end. I do think I'll be sad if I die without seeing Haputa again, but my home is here now, close to Quip. Dowlin has been a fine friend to me, Quip delightfully funny, and the city is a beautiful place to live. I never thought to see a place like it, much less spend the rest of my life here.

LYRAH

The Warrior

Year 111, 56th day of winter

Trill's wedding is today, and I couldn't be happier for her. I guess that this means she'll not be returning to Haputa. I won't be either then. Funny, that Haputa is my country, my one love really, and I shan't live there again. But if Trill is queen of Laitmea, I'll stay by her side. It's not all her, though. There is this rather dashing Captain of the Guard, who I hope to see today…

Maybe my feelings are becoming a little clearer on the matter. Redge is well, all those silly romantic things Lara would say about Donis, except he's not a feckless little snob.

* * *

Later

I guess Redge was jealous after seeing Dowlin kiss Trill so many times, and had to take it out on me. We talked at great length, about Trill and Dowlin, and Ettalara and Donis, and about us. He misses Haputa too, but agrees that since all the people we love are here, there's nothing for it but to stay. Whatever else passed between us is not fit for writing. We didn't get to pleasantries in a heartbeat, and there was ample time for profanity before we worked out our differences. Things smoothed over quickly enough, however. There was dancing too, It being a wedding and all. Trill's dress was so pretty, and we laughed our heads off with how besotted Donis is with Lara, then again when I noticed that Redge had the same look on his face. I hope that's not what I look like now, even though there's no one here to see. I think I'm falling in love, which other than being inconvenient and embarrassing is really quite nice.

The Lady

56th Day of Winter

Trill was wed to Dowlin today! It was a most beautiful ceremony. Trill wore a dress of white with tiny diamonds stitched onto her skirt. Her hair was swept up into an elegant braided style and she wore a puffy white veil that hung from her tiara. (It took a great deal of convincing to get her to put all of this on and Quip only narrowly kept her from climbing a tree to escape.) In the end though, the wedding came off without a hitch. There were lots of rich pastries and cakes and, of course, ice cream. The dancing included everything from waltzes to schottisches. (I think Trill only tolerated slow dances because it gave her time to "borrow" things from her dancing partners.) Anyway, it's quite late and so I think I shall end for now.

Redgenold

56th of Winter, year 111

  At last Quip has given in and accepted my manifold apologies. We had a grand time at the wedding after the necessary unpleasantries were out of the way. Quip has a sharp tongue, and managed to lay open every old wound I possess with it, but then I deserve some verbal flogging now and again. I could feel the old whiplash scars on her back when we danced, from more than one physical flogging, and I knew that I was right to kill the slave driver, even if my motives were not pure. She leaned her head on my chest for the slow dances, and cursed etiquette in terms that should never be written down. I made her laugh with my speculations about corsets, and we wished a pox upon fashion as a whole, and did a set of dances barefoot. Trill scolded us for it, saying we should have done it sooner, and Ettalara buried her face in the tablecloth and wept at the impropriety of it all.

The Thief

Year 111, 57th day of winter

My wedding was yesterday. Funny enough, I was more nervous for that short little ceremony than I've ever been for anything else in my life. In my nervousness, I accidentally swiped the ring Dowlin was supposed to give me, but I managed to get it back to its right place before even Dowlin noticed. Other than that, things were kind of a blur. Quip hugged me and insisted on a celebratory piece of cake before the reception. (We cut it from the back, so no one could tell). Lara cried through the whole ceremony, which was very annoying and yet slightly comforting, too. It's nice that at least someone can act semi-normal at important events. She did give me a lovely necklace as a gift (I already knew about it because I swiped it last week before I realized what it was). It's actually really nice, not too flashy, but not too boring, either. Quip gave me our old book of etiquette and a couple of matches and Dowlin and I spent our first night together curled up in bed watching the cozy flames slowly devour that torturous book. All in all it was a good day!

* * *

58th day of winter

I almost panicked this morning, waking up next to Dowlin. He was still sound asleep. I gave him a gentle poke, but all he did was snore, so I picked up my truncheon from the bedside table, and rapped on his shoulder. That woke him up!

Not much going on today but preparations for the Coronation. I think I'll give Dart a bath. He's still technically Haputian property, but nobody is brave enough to try to make him leave me. He has grown so large that we've had to construct a new pen, and his saliva now catches on fire regularly. I think there's a line about him in one of the treaties. Anyway, none of the Senators has had any control over him since I called him to the Capitol to take our message back to Haputa. Apparently, he flew back and dropped my message on their heads and then turned right around and came to roost in Lara's stables and scared all the horses half to death. I can't imagine what a shock it must have been for them. (The Senators, not the horses- well, them too.)

So now that Dart is no longer Haputa's war Dragon he's just a very big pet who likes to eat whole cows. I wonder if he feels as useless as I sometimes do? Like just another pretty (or scaly in his case) face to look at.

* * *

59th day of winter

Coronation Day! I get a gold crown with rubies on it, like a smaller version of Dowlin's. All I have to do to get it is walk into the throne room looking serious, and pledge my undying loyalty to Laitmea with the same archaic wording that every king and queen has used for about a million years. It's a tall order though, and when I rehearsed it over and over yesterday, Quip kept laughing at about the third *"hath pledged".*

Redgenold

59th of Winter, year 111

Dowlin and Trill were crowned today. Quip found the ceremony enormously funny, but I found it rather moving.

The Warrior

Year 111, 59th day of winter

Trill held it together for the coronation. I did not. "I hath pledged myself to the service of mine country." Honestly.

* * *

Year 111, 60th day of winter

I was in court today, to see the last land given back. I recognized the Haputian senators, who seemed a little sheepish after not trusting Trill and me. I must say that I didn't understand aught of what went on, but Trill wanted me there in case the Czar tried anything, and she needed an extra knife. Redge was guarding king Dowlin, and kept winking at me, and making me come over all funny and start blushing when I was supposed to be sitting up straight and serious. I honestly don't know why he's started having this effect on me, but if this is how he felt around me all those years, I pity the poor chap. I don't know what I'd do, seeing him strut around behind Dowlin all the time, not being able to say anything to him.

* * *

Year 111,61st day of winter

I was rather ill this morning, so much I couldn't come to court to see off the last of the diplomats of other countries. Just when I thought I was done for, Redge burst in all upset that I hadn't been there, and I was so glad that somebody had pity on me that I forgot to box his ears and slap his face. I was feeling rather better by the time he professed his love to me again, (The two things are utterly unrelated, I swear it) But he wasn't done there. I was actually pleased when he asked me to marry him, but rather than show it, I demanded that he fetch the doctor at once, and not the one living across the way from us. (I still stay with Ettalara, Trill is in the palace now). I insisted that he bring the medic who treated me for plague on the pirate's ship. It isn't plague, I'm sure, but I liked that medic, and it got Redge out of the way for quite some time so I could think. I'm still thinking now.

* * *

Year 111, 62nd day of winter

To my utter amazement, Redge managed to track the man down. He has just left, and I am chewing on some foul tasting herbs that are supposed to calm my stomach if I'm taken ill again. He was in the Capitol, (which is why it only took Redge two hours to find him instead of two weeks). I learned that the medic was the brother of Mer's diplomat, in town for the signing of treaties. When I had asked Redge for the doctor, he went running off, and gained so much momentum that he knocked over the ambassador and the poor man landed on a drink cart in the lobby of his inn. Redge then barged in on the medic taking a bath. The diplomat will take some convincing not to pull out of the treaty after "that idiot swordsman!" but I don't doubt Trill will manage him. I am really quite glad that it happened, for the medic has made up my mind. He quite bluntly said that I should marry Redge. As he put it "The boy loves you terribly. If you don't accept, and soon, there will be many repeats of today's idiotic episode." I truly can't leave Redge to blunder into any more dignitaries. For that, and other reasons I blush too much about to write of, I shall accept his proposal. But only after I hit him for being such a ninny.

302

Redgenold

62nd of Winter, year 111

Quip gave me quite a turn yesterday. She wasn't in court, and when I came to call upon her and Ettalara, I found her abed in a frightful condition. Having no experience doctoring the ill, I offered my sympathies and asked her to be mine in marriage. Why ever I did so is beyond me- I love her, but calling the doctor would have made more sense. When she demanded a pirates' medic, I dashed off, on what I feared was a wild goose chase, but after half and an hour of fruitless searching, I learned that the man was residing at an inn on the opposite side of town. I dare say I knocked a few men over in my mad dash to reach him- but in the end I found him and he treated Quip and all was forgotten. To my astonishment, Quip has accepted my proposal, so we shall be wed just as soon as all is in order.

The Thief

62nd day of winter

Quip and Redge are getting married. Quip! To Redge! Even after all that's happened, I can hardly believe it. Ah, love is in the air. Or something. Why is love never in the water? Or the ground?

* * *

63rd day of winter

Death, death, double death to anyone who suggests that silk stockings are practical. I want ice cream!

The Lady

63rd Day of Winter

Redge proposed to Quip! They are to be married sometime in the spring. I never thought I would live to see the day when Quip would settle down. Much less with Redge. Oh, I do love poetic justice!

Redgenold

70th of winter, year 111

It is an odd thing that every man my age is searching for a wife, or is newly wed. In the Haputian countryside, one gets married when one can- here there is no such stalling. Without crops to plant or harvests to bring in, one's only duty is to find a spouse as soon as one is of age.

The Warrior

Year 111,78th day of winter

My own wedding plans are starting. Good grief, the whole thing has to be Laitmean? If I'd have known the kind of wedding gowns they wear here, I wouldn't have agreed to stay for Trill!!!!

* * *

Year 111,81st day of winter

A pox upon the house of Thiefdom! Trill has made off with my jeweled tiara, which I was meaning to wear next week. I must steal it back before then, which will be hard, as she has a dragon to guard it.

The Thief

82nd day of winter

Quip is in the midst of their own wedding plans. She came over to the palace today to commiserate with me about dresses and teacups and dance steps. I offered to sneak out and go dragon riding with her, but then a Lord from some prestigious family came to complain about something, so we couldn't go.

The Lady

Year 110, 1st Day of Spring

Today I returned home. It is lovely to be back, but somehow all I can think of is how my parents ought to be here. I expected to feel happy, and I do, but more than anything, I feel as though I've left something behind.

When I left here, I was still in shock, a girl terrified of what awaited her. Now I return a young woman, and while the pain and fear have faded, the lessons I've learned have been sobering, and the reality I now face is anything but cheering. I thought regaining my fortune would make everything all right again, but I see now that if it had been at the cost of friendship or experience, it would have meant nothing. Quip and Trill, crass and uncivilized as they were at times, taught me more than I ever learned within these walls. Loyalty and bravery are worth more than I ever could have imagined. While we may never truly see eye to eye, leaving them has been a test of strength.

Yes, I wanted to leave, and return to what is rightfully mine, but I also needed to leave. I need to be out of Dowlin and Trill's way, as they rebuild the country and build their family. As much as I hate it, I need to be out of Donis' way as well. Perhaps, someday, when we are both grown up, it will work out, but for now, I can see no future for us. Funny, that I always thought coming of age would make me grown up, but the older I get, the more I see how I am not.

I am almost to the end of this diary, but I will not continue to fill it with these dreary musings. I will save the last pages to write a suitable conclusion, when I am less muddled and heartbroken.

Redgenold

1st of spring, year 110

Ettalara returned to her home today. Despite what one might think, I have been a little sad to see her go. Quip of course would not admit to such a thing, but after having lived through both slavery and pirate attack with someone, you don't forget them in a hurry. Then again, Quip did not live through the pirates so much as facilitate their piracy.

The Warrior

Year 110, 1st day of spring

Hurrah and Huzzah! Ettalara is gone! Now Trill and I can get on with our lives. Admittedly, I may miss her a bit, but not so much as I'll miss tormenting her. Sometimes she just needed it. I'll roast some crickets in honor of her departure, and drink her a toast from my flagon of cockroach wine!

(Actually, I just gave her a hug and good wishes.)

The Thief

1st day of spring, year 110 (110!)

Ettalara has left. Well, Quip might say good riddance, but we went through a lot together. An orphanage, a slave camp, pirates, fussy dinner parties and assassinations. Maybe the best we could ever manage was grudging respect, but in the end, I like to think we parted friends.

Redgenold

13th of spring, year 110

Without a war, the Captain of Laitmeas' guard and bodyguard to the king and queen has not much to do, so I have not written of late. I put this down now, for tomorrow is my wedding. I shan't sleep a wink- As we shall be married in the palace, Quip is in the room next to mine, and I can hear her snoring.

The Warrior

Year 110,14th day of Spring

I'm in hysterics, waiting to be married, but I'm nothing next to Redge. I saw him last yesterday morn, and he was trembling like a leaf. I teased him mercilessly for it. It helps me deal with the nerves.

The Thief

14th day of spring

Quip and Redge! I still can't believe it. Quip better though!

The Warrior

Year 110, 15th day of spring

Success! Redge is a married man, and neither of us tripped over our feet during the ceremony. Now I must wake Redge up to begin our first day together. This may prove a difficult task, as he has been known to sleep through battles. I borrowed Trill's truncheon especially for the occasion.

REDGENOLD

Redgenold

15th of spring, year 110

I was drunk for the second time in my life yesterday- after the wedding, of course. Such a rowdy and happy gathering has never been seen. Trill trained Dart of Doom to dance for the occasion, and the dragon has a talent for fireworks which awed the guests. Both of us may be orphans, but we've found our family now.

The Warrior

Year 110, 18th day of spring

My allotted year is up. I'll save the last few pages for any monumental events to come. Like children, or dogs, or maybe an out of place doily. Life is proving to be pretty boring without war and espionage to keep me busy. Redge had better watch his back, for I feel a sudden urge to beat someone to a pulp.

The Thief

20th day of spring

 I'm sixteen today! Dowlin has been showering me with presents, even a few that I didn't already know about, like a new scrub brush for Dart. (He ate the last one.) Quip gave me a pail of ice cream. She's been acting a little odd recently, I hope nothing's wrong. She doesn't seem to have nearly the appetite for violence that she usually does.

Redgenold

44th of spring, year 110

Quip is going to have a child! If ever there is more to this story, it is my son or daughters to write down now. I shall put this book away soon- perhaps I shall send it to my Uncle after all. He never saw my mother again, but he might want to know of her descendants.

The Warrior

Year 110,44th day of spring

Speaking of monumental... A Child!

I shall be free of my corset for a while, not that one would do much anyway. Redge has been walking into walls from joy. Why does he do that? For some reason strong emotions make him lose all coordination. It does explain why I could always best him in fights, though. Against someone he's not in love with, he's almost unbeatable.

The Thief

45th Day of spring

I've been writing less and less frequently, but there's been less and less going on. But this is something: Quip having a baby. I hope the little one knows what it's in for with a mother like that! I love Quip, but sometimes she can be a bit, how to put it, exuberant? Maybe a bit too exuberant?

* * *

55th day of spring

This is the last page of this diary. I've been skimming through my entries, and am struck by how short a time it was in which everything changed. This time last year I was only Trill, the Haputian thief, and now here I am, sixteen years old, married, and queen of Laitmea. Who would have thought it?

For the most part, I'm happy with the way things turned out. I'm married to the most wonderful man in the world, who knows my background and faults (I still swipe things from him, often out of habit) and loves me anyway. Quip is going to stay here with me. Is there anything better than living in the same palace as your best friend? I don't think so, but keeping a pet dragon and having my own personal ice cream cook do come close.

Ettalara's not too far away either. I'm glad I don't have to see her every day, but if she had moved very far away, I think a part of me would have been a little sad.

The best news of all, of course, is news that I have yet to tell even my friends. I'm going to have an heir to the throne soon! I'm beyond ecstatic but have decided to keep it quiet until a little closer to time. I don't want everyone fussing over me for the entire time. Mine will be only a little younger than Quip's. Maybe our children can be friends when they grow up!

The only thing I shall miss is Haputa. I will always consider it my home, even though I don't even live there anymore. But all is not lost. If the queen is ever sick and refuses to come out of her room or see anyone for a week or so, you may guess where I'll be.

On Life

I once met a man
Who sailed the blue sea
Chains had cut him deep
But strength set him free
Brands had burned his flesh
And stones hit his head
Whips had cut his back
And left him for dead
Scars were on his hands
And on his face too
He walked with a limp
His legs black and blue
But he said to me
I live a good life
I have had some troubles
And my share of strife
But for many a man
Life is but a dream
A reflection of nightmares
Smoke seen through a screen
I have lived so full

And for so many years
Sucked the marrow from life
And shed so many tears
That I'd say I'm lucky
To have lived at all
My joys have been great
And my sorrows so small
I asked him for more
And he laughed and said
Live son and live deeply
Or you're better off dead

Redgenold

59th of fall, year 110
   A continuation of my last entry-

To my Uncle Efin,
   I appreciate your response. I am sure that were she alive, my mother would have no hard feelings towards you.
   Your great niece was born yesterday. She is as beautiful as her mother, with corn floss golden hair and eyes the color of the sea- Which according to my late mother, are just what yours look like- that pretty bluish green. I hope this finds you well,
   Your loving nephew,
   Redge.

Warrior

Troublesome is what they call a girl of rowdy disposition,
Worthless is the word for one of somewhat low position.
Ugly- if her eyes are flint and her tongue is made of steel
Selfish, they all say of her, as if she cannot feel.
If she cannot sit up straight, wear dresses and act sweet,
Why then, she might as well be thrown out in the street.
There cannot be room in a gentleman's heart
For a girl who is rowdy and bitter and tart.
A sharp kind of wit will do her no good
If she cannot be pretty in the way that she should.
If her gift is for tactics, why that is a shame,
For girls can't play war-That's a man's game.
If your prickly stick to sewing and you'll see,
The parlor's where a woman ought to be.
But if you see a certain soldier with an awful lot of pluck
Who time and time again leaves her fate to luck,
They told her no, they tried to hold her back-
It seems she has the sense all others lack.
She proved them wrong, and now she holds her head up proud and high.
A girl can be a warrior, if she's not afraid to die.

The Warrior

Year 110, 60th day of fall

The monumental event being that I am in love.

Some thoughts, not that writing about emotions has done me any good in the past, but I think this time is different. It's more for reflection than sorting things out.

I suppose it stands to reason. I only saw the Redgenold I wanted to see. He was always a lot smarter than I thought he was.

The battle between Laitmea and Haputa was never as black and white as I tried to believe. I always thought that protecting someone smaller gave you the right to do a lot of really awful things to the people who were bigger. I guess I was sort of the bully.

Lara was never really evil, but she's still a snob.

And Trill really does deserve to be queen, even if it's not in her birth country. She and Dowlin get along so well, and I guess in the end she certainly was the least horrid of all of us. Donis is a cry baby, and Dowlin is a cold blooded killer, but he did stop the war. And then there's Redge. He's actually not bad. In fact, he's really great. Maybe, just maybe, I was so, so wrong about him. For one thing, he's an amazing dancer. And he is smart. I mean, we dumped him in Laitmea out of a boat with nothing but the clothes on his back, and in a few seasons he was the captain of the guard. He does love me. Apparently he always has. I hope he always will. I'm still a warrior at heart, but with him around, I don't feel so silly acting like a Lady. It's nice not to have to constantly prove that I'm strong, 'cause he already knows it. (He better with the way I used to beat him!)

This book is almost full up, so there's just enough room for a little bit about me.

My name is Quipeneay, I'm sixteen, and I live in the palace of Laitmea. I'm a bodyguard for the queen, my best friend Trill. I still like fire, but I've cut back on stealing things. Mostly I love my family and friends. I probably won't keep a diary again, because I'm really too busy to write in it. I have a baby daughter, who I named Trilliapa-Ettalara. Mostly Redge and I call her Lara, since Trill is a much more popular name here in Laitmea now that Trill the elder is queen. She has a little daughter too now, with gold hair and blue eyes, and little princess Addmaleta is keeping her so busy that I don't think she writes anymore either. BEST FRIENDS FOREVER!!!!!!!!!!!!!!

6

10 What is a Lady?
Is a Lady a person well dressed, well groomed?
Is she pretty and witty and well to do?
Is she noble of birth and bearing,
A gem of society not worth comparing?
When seeing a Lady, must on assess
Her deportment and smile as well as her dress?
A Lady is a woman of courage strength,
A person who would go to any length
To stand up for what is right and good,
No matter if others say that she should.
A Lady never ever leaves a friend,
She stays beside them until the end.
A Lady is intelligent and bold and kind,
She is the best sort of person that any could find.

Epilogue

Three years later...

The Lady

Year 107, 8th Day of Summer

I have saved the last pages of this book in order to write a suitable conclusion, which I shall do now. I returned to my home in high spirits, but not as elated as I might have been. Despite what I wrote, I truly did not *want* to wait to marry Donis, even if the time allowed him to mature considerably.

Rather than pine away over him, I found the faithful servants who helped me the weeks following my parents' deaths and rewarded each of them with a large sum of money. They have all bought small homes and retired and seem to be living quite comfortably.

After I felt that a suitable length of time had elapsed, I began again to write to Donis, and soon afterword to visit him regularly. I also visited Trill and Quip, who showed differing levels of enthusiasm for our little chats. (Two guesses who tried to throw me out of her house!)

Perhaps I was lonely, seeing them both settle down, but my relationship with Donis soon blossomed into love. Despite my vow not to write any more in this little book, I found some things too good not to record. I shall copy them down here:

Donis wrote me a song! He played his mandolin and sang it to me this evening. The lyrics were so beautiful and I wish I could write them down, but I'm fairly certain that Quip and Trill sneak peaks at my diary quite often and so I shall not copy it here. I am not at all being biased when I say that Donis has a lovely voice and great musical talent. Now I am glad for those harpsichord lessons Mother made me take!

Quip had a daughter, Trill had a daughter, and soon after Quip had a son. I would not be surprised if they both have many more children in the future. Finally, Donis proposed. Once again, I kept a small record for myself:

It is only a matter of days before I shall wed Donis. I am excited, but also nervous and a little bit sad. I'm leaving one stage of life and entering into another. I suppose that's bound to make one feel a little sad.

The wedding preparations are coming along nicely. The wedding is to take place at the palace, but we shall go to my home after the ceremony for the reception.

I tried on my wedding dress today! It is a lovely, simple white gown with a skirt that touches the floor and a thick white sash around the waist. There is lace around the neckline and pearl buttons down the back and the sleeves are made of see-through white lace. I have a lovely long veil, not nearly as puffy as Trill's, attached to my tiara and I shall carry a bouquet of pink and yellow flowers.

These are happy memories, of course, that I do not wish to forget, but I also want to keep a record of my accomplishments, good and ill. There were times I wanted very much to forget my own foibles, but in retrospect I am glad that I have kept this journal. If there is anything I have learned from it, it is not to think too highly of myself, or to judge others too swiftly.

Donis and I are still living in my home quite happily. We are now nineteen. We had our first child last month, a boy named Donis Cornelius Atticus III after his father and grandfather. We just threw in the Atticus for good measure.

So far, Trill has made a good queen and Dowlin a good king. She has by no means changed; every time she comes over for a visit she takes a silver spoon or gold watch. I guess old habits are hard to break. We are finally at peace with Haputa, largely thanks to Trill's treaties, and have restored to them (and other countries) their land.

I suppose that my final reason for this conclusion is to remark that I shall always have the correct account of how the events actually unfolded. (Quip and Trill's accounts, sadly, are not always the most accurate, despite their claims to the contrary.)

Until I next set out to write, I remain faithfully yours,

Princess Ettalara Annalee of Laitmea.

ETTALARA'S
HOUSE

How to read the poems

And now that our tale has come to a close,
You may have been wondering about our prose.
Perhaps all the numbers just didn't make sense,
(And their constant occurrence made you quite tense).
Perhaps if you think on the story just told,
And ponder the riddle of that book so old,
Which was solved in this story by Trill and Quip,
The answer will come to you quick as a sip
Of the poison that murdered that nasty old king.
Count all your words if sweet triumph you'd sing.

1: Irony.
   13: The.

2: Upon the Sea.
   100: Treasure.

3: Just Desserts?
   16: Of.

4: The Lady.

31: Laitmean.

5: Sail, if you like.
   35: Kings.

6: What is a Lady?
   10: Is.

7: Thief!
   4: Kept.

8: The Iceman.
   100: In.
   101: The.

9: In the woods I stand.
   47: Forest.

10: Your secret is safe with me.
   20: Guarded.

11: The Stars.
   19: By.

12: For the love of Gunpowder.
   135: Cannon.

13: The Knight.
   30:Where.
   93: Only.

14: Snow.
   49: A.

15: The Hunt.
  42: Dragon.

16: How could you?
  56: Could.

17: ii, The Beast.
  16: Find.

18: The Pickpocket.
  54: It.

Pronunciation Guide

Eretz (Air-ets) (âr' ĕts): The continent on which our story takes place.

Mer (MER) (mĭ' r): The land of the pirates.

Onkay (On-KAY)(än kā'): The desert land.

Styllyg (Still-igg) (stĭl' ĭg): The land of the long grass.

Laitmea (Lay-it-may-ah) (lā' ĭt mā' ŭ): The largest country in the land of Eretz.

Lyrah (LIE-rah) (lī' rä): The capital of Laitmea.

Donis (Daw-niss)(dâ' nĭs): The youngest Laitmean prince.

Dowlin (Dow-lin)(dou lĭn'): The crown prince of Laitmea.

Elisabet (Elis-U-bett) (ē' lĭs ä' bĕt): The late queen of Laitmea, Donis and Dowlin's' mother.

Ettalara (Eta-lara)(ĕtû' lärä): A Laitmean noble woman.

Hillena (Hill-enn-AH) (hĭl' ĕ nä): Ettalara's mother.

Haputa (Huh-poo-tuh)(hŭ' poo' tŭ): The smallest country in the land of Eretz.

Archon (ARE-ch-ON) (är' ch ăn'): The capital of Haputa.

Quirton (Kw-ER-tun)(kw ûr' tŭn): A town near the Haputian border with Laitmea.

Quipeneay/ Quip (QUIP-in-YAY) (kwĭp' ĭn yā): An orphan from Haputa.

Evayah (Uh-vay-uh) (ŭ vā' ä): A false name adopted by Quipeneay.

Redgenold/ Redge (Redge-un-old) (rĕg' ŭ' nōld): A Haputian orphan, the son of an assassin.

Efin (ef- IN) (ĕf ĭn'): Redgenold's uncle.

Trilliapa/ Trill (trill-ee-yupa) (trĭl ē' ŭpä) : A Haputian thief.

Addmaleta (ADD-ma-LEE-ta) (ăd' mä lētä) : A false name adopted by Trilliapa.

Brone (Berr-OWN) (brōn): Trilliapas' father, a disgraced senator.

Acknowledgment

BelaJane here,

Well, one would think that self publishing would mean fewer people to thank. Nope. They'd be very wrong.

First, I shall thank my parents, for supporting me, and not questioning my bizarre explanations of the plot. It got better as it went along, but there were some weird stops along the way. I'm glad I cut the mermaid incident.

Those who read this book first also deserve some serious thanking. Amanda, Ann, Anna, Claire, and Gwen. Of the many I sent the manuscript to, you actually responded, and gave constructive criticism. THANK YOU!

Then there are those who added to my kickstarter campaign. You were promised a book with your name in it, and here it is: In no particular order,

Andrea Zachotina, Daniele, Caelin Johnson, Jim L, Joanne, Angel R. York,

J. Jasper, John Adams, Lauren Sutter, Daria Skrzypczynski,

Peter & Judy Smith, Steve, Julie B, Anna Fisher Aimee Dowgwillo,

Gerald Buttice, Tanisha, Kristina Gsedl, and of course, Oma, Opa, and Grandma!

Thanks upon thanks. I hope you love it! You helped make it happen.

In conclusion, no book is just an author. Even one as silly as this has a lot of people behind it, and they all deserve to have their name in print. (If you don't usually read the acknowledgments, please take this as the threat it is. Be nice to the people at the back of the book. They're there for a reason.)

And just remember, if ever you're having a bad day, you can be thankful that your name isn't Dowlin.

Thus endeth the book.

About the Author

BelaJane Crilly is the author of several halfway decent fantasy novels. She lives outside of Chicago, and currently attends college for several subjects only tangentially related to creative writing. Her loved ones frequently accuse her of 'selling herself short' but this is her bio and she can say whatever she likes.

You can connect with me on:

- https://belajanebooks.weebly.com
- https://twitter.com/belajanecrilly
- https://www.instagram.com/belajanecrilly

Also by BelaJane Crilly

Coming Soon!

Twenty years after Laitmeas' surrender, echos of their war with Haputa still remain. Now the tides are shifting, and discontent is on the rise. Famine tears through Onkay, and the pirates are restless in their haunts. If the still fledgling peace between neighboring countries is to last, Laitmeas' king and queen must remain strong. Yet they may be in the most danger of all…